THE GIRL
WHO WAS
SUPPOSED
TO DIE

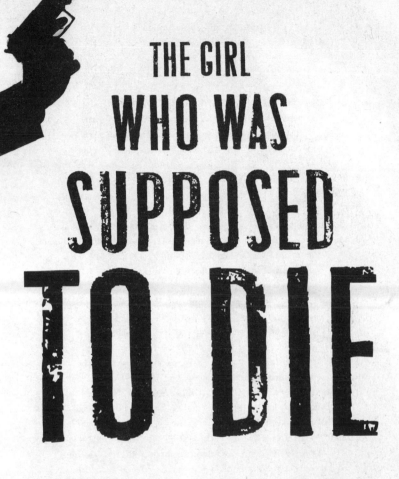

THE GIRL
WHO WAS
SUPPOSED
TO DIE

APRIL HENRY

SQUARE
FISH

Henry Holt and Company

NEW YORK

SQUARE
FISH

An Imprint of Macmillan
175 Fifth Avenue
New York, NY 10010
macteenbooks.com

Square Fish books may be purchased for business or promotional use. For information on bulk purchases, please contact the Macmillan Corporate and Premium Sales Department at (800) 221-7945 x5442 or by e-mail at specialmarkets@macmillan.com.

Library of Congress Cataloging-in-Publication Data
Henry, April.
The girl who was supposed to die / April Henry.
pages cm
Summary: "She doesn't know who she is. She doesn't know where she is, or why. All she knows when she comes to in a ransacked cabin is that there are two men arguing over whether or not to kill her. And that she must run.
Follow Cady and Ty (her accidental savior turned companion), as they race against the clock to stay alive." —Provided by publisher.
ISBN 978-1-250-04437-2 (paperback) / ISBN 978-0-8050-9903-4 (e-book)
[1. Amnesia—Fiction.   2. Adventure and adventurers—Fiction.
3. Survival—Fiction.   4. Biological warfare—Fiction.   5. Identity theft—Fiction.   6. Mystery and detective stories.]   I. Title.
PZ7.H39356Giu 2013   [Fic]—dc23   2013001698

Originally published in the United States by
Christy Ottaviano Books/Henry Holt and Company
First Square Fish Edition: 2014
Book designed by April Ward
Square Fish logo designed by Filomena Tuosto

1 3 5 7 9 10 8 6 4 2

AR: 4.7 / LEXILE: HL690L

*Dedicated to the memory
of Bridget Zinn (1977–2011),
writer, librarian, friend, wife—
a vibrant woman who could make
an ordinary day into an occasion*

CHAPTER 1

DAY 1, 4:51 P.M.

I wake up.

But wake up isn't quite right. That implies sleeping. A bed. A pillow.

I come to.

Instead of a pillow, my right cheek is pressed against something hard, rough, and gritty. A worn wood floor.

My mouth tastes like old pennies. Blood. With my eyes still closed, I gently touch my teeth with my tongue. One of them feels loose. The inside of my mouth is shredded and sore. My head aches and there's a faint buzzing in one ear.

And something is wrong with my left hand. The tips of my pinkie and ring finger throb with every beat of my heart. The pain is sharp and red.

Two men are talking, their voices a low murmur. Something about no one coming for me. Something about it's too late.

I decide to keep my eyes closed. Not to move. I'm not sure I could anyway. It's not only my tooth that feels wrong.

Footsteps move closer to me. A shoe kicks me in the ribs. Not very hard. More like a nudge. Still, I don't allow myself to react. Through slitted eyes, I see two pairs of men's shoes. One pair of brown boots and one pair of red-brown dress shoes that shade to black on the toes. A distant part of me thinks the color is called oxblood.

"She doesn't know anything," a man says. He doesn't sound angry or even upset. It's a simple statement of fact.

I realize he's right. I don't know anything. What's wrong with me, where I am, who they are. And when I try to think about who I am, what I get is: nothing. A big gray hole. All I know for sure is that I must be in trouble.

"I need to get back to Portland and follow our leads there," the other man says. "You need to take care of things here. Take her out back and finish her off."

"But she's just a kid," the first man says. His tone is not quite so neutral now.

"A kid?" The second man's voice hardens. "If she talks to the cops, she could get us both sent to death row. It's either her or us. It's that simple." His footsteps move away from me. "Call me when you're done."

The other man nudges me with his foot again. A little harder this time.

Behind me, I hear a door open and close.

"Come on. Get up." With a sigh, he leans over and grabs me under my arms. Grunting, he hauls me up from behind. His breath smells bitter, like coffee. I try to keep my body limp, but when my left hand brushes the floor, the

8

pain in my fingers is an electric shock. My legs stiffen and he pulls me to my feet.

"That's right," he says, nudging me forward while still holding me up. "We're going to take a little walk."

Since he already knows that I'm conscious, I figure I can open my eyes halfway. We're in what looks like a cabin, with knotty pine walls and a black wood-burning stove. Yellow stuffing spills from sliced cushions on an old plaid couch and a green high-backed chair. Books lie splayed below an emptied bookcase. Someone was obviously looking for something, but I don't know what, and I don't know if they found it. Past the red-and-white-checkered curtains lie nothing but fir trees.

With the guy's arm clamped around my shoulders, I stumble past a table with four wood chairs. One of them is turned away from the table. Ropes loosely encircle the arms. A pair of bloody pliers sits on the table next to what seems like two silver-white chips mostly painted pink.

I look down at my limp left hand. Pink polish on three of the nails. The tips of the last two fingers are wet and red where nails used to be.

I think I know where I was before I ended up on the floor.

I keep every step small and shuffling so that he's half carrying me. It's not easy because he's not much bigger than me, maybe five foot nine. The guy mutters under his breath, but that's all. Maybe he doesn't want to get to where we are going any more than I do. The back door is about twenty feet away.

Outside, a car starts up and then drives away. The only

other sounds are the wind in the trees outside and the man grunting every now and then as he tries to make my body walk in a straight line.

Wherever we are, I think we're alone. It's just me and this guy. And once he manages to get me out the door, he'll follow instructions.

He'll finish me off.

Kill me.

CHAPTER 2

DAY 1, 4:54 P.M.

We keep walking toward the back door of the cabin. Except the guy holding me up is doing most of the walking. My left knee bangs into the nearest chair. I don't lift my feet, letting my toes drag on the floor. I'm trying to buy myself some time. Trying to figure out how to save myself. My half-closed eyes flick from side to side, looking for a weapon. Looking for anything that could help me. But there's no iron poker next to the woodstove, no knives on the counter, no old-fashioned black telephone on the wall. Just gaping drawers and emptied-out cupboards and a big mess on the floor—cookie sheets and cans and dishtowels and boxes of cereal and crackers that have been upended and shaken empty.

He has to take one hand away from me to open the door. *Don't act. Be,* a voice whispers inside my head. I picture my consciousness dwindling. I let my body go limp, and slide from his grasp. It's tough to stay slack when my fingertips hit the rough wood. The pain arcs up my arm like I just stuck my fingers in a light socket. Still, I keep tumbling loosely to the floor as if I'm completely out.

Playing dead. Hoping I won't *be* dead soon. Maybe if he thinks I'm unconscious, he'll let his guard down.

With a sigh, the man steps over me, and kicks the door open, letting in a wave of cold air. He leans down and rolls me over so that I'm face up again. It's so hard not to stiffen, especially as every bit of me feels tender and bruised, but I bite my tongue and try to remain loose. Then he grabs me under the arms and begins to drag me backward, grunting at every step. His chin brushes the top of my head.

He can't see my face. I wonder if that's a mistake. It will be easier to kill me if he doesn't have to look into my pleading eyes. Doesn't have to see my lips tremble as I beg for my life.

My feet thump over the sill. I open my eyes again. I see a worn earthen path stretching back to the cabin, my feet in blue Nike running shoes, my legs in skinny jeans. Reddish brown stains splotch the thighs. I wonder if the blood is only from my fingers.

I let my hands, even the broken one, trail along the ground. Under my fingertips, I feel cold earth, ridged with footprints, muddy in spots. A stick about as big around as one of my fingers. And then my good hand closes on a rock, small enough to fit into my palm, rounded on one side, with one sharp edge.

If this man has a gun—which seems more than

likely—the rock won't help me much. Even David had the help of a sling when he used a stone to kill Goliath.

The going is easier now. Pine trees surround us and my heels slide over copper-colored needles. I can't imagine this guy, who by now is breathing heavily, will drag me for miles and miles. Soon he'll drop me, take out his more-than-likely gun, and shoot me in the head. Or the heart. Or maybe both.

I'm going to die and I don't know why.

I don't even know who I am.

I wonder if he'll bother to bury me. Or maybe he'll just leave my body for whatever lives in these woods.

No! The thought is so fierce I have to clamp my lips together to keep from shouting it. I can't wait for *him* to choose what happens to me. I can't just wait for him to kill me.

He's dragging me past a small tree. I stick out one leg and hook my foot around the trunk. We jerk to a stop.

"Come on now." He sighs. "Let's not make this harder than it has to be."

He lifts me to reposition his grip. I manage to get my feet under me. He's so close his breath stirs the hair on the nape of my neck.

I don't know what I'm going to do until suddenly I'm doing it. My right elbow drives back like a piston, landing square in his belly. He grunts in an explosion of air and starts to fold up. The bottom of my right fist is already swinging down to hammer his groin. And then I swing my hand up, twisting it until the back of my fist hits him square in the face. Hard. And made even harder by the rock I hold in my hand. Under my knuckles, I feel the bridge of his nose crack.

I spin around to face him. His eyes are half closed in pain. Blood runs from his nose, red as paint. His right hand reaches out to grab me. My left hand rises, bent at the wrist like the neck of a crane, and knocks his hand away. Then my hand snaps back and claws down, fingers spread, my remaining fingernails digging into his cheeks, leaving furrows that immediately fill with blood. He cries out and puts his hands to his face.

Leaving his throat unprotected. I draw back my hand, my fingers close together and bent at the second knuckle. And I drive them into his throat as hard as I can.

And then he's lying flat on his back, not moving.

I'm not sure he's even breathing.

All my moves were automatic. I didn't have to think. Didn't have to remember anything.

Whoever I am, I already know how to do this.

CHAPTER 3

DAY 1, 4:58 P.M.

The guy who was going to kill me is lying on the ground, silent and still.

Now what do I do?

My first instinct is to run.

But I'm pretty sure he has a gun. What if he wakes up? He could shoot me before I even make it back to the cabin.

I nudge his shoulder with my foot, ready to jump back if he moves. But he doesn't. He's a white guy, maybe thirty or a little older, slender and on the short side, with thick black hair cut very short. He's wearing dark jeans and a black soft-shell jacket with a hood. His eyes are half open, his mouth slack.

Is he dead?

I kick him in the side about the same way he kicked me. Without a lot of conviction.

He still doesn't move. But he's definitely breathing.

Although it's not exactly breathing. It's more like gasping. Ragged and uneven.

But at least he's not dead.

I lean over him, my heart racing. I can feel every beat in my ears, in the hollow of my throat, in my mangled fingertips. I'm so afraid he's going to sit up and grab me.

I have to find his gun. But what if I'm wrong about what he was going to do? What if he doesn't even have a gun? Because I think I've really hurt him. Maybe I didn't understand what I heard. Maybe I didn't understand what I saw. Maybe there is a different explanation for what was happening, and it doesn't involve him killing me.

Maybe.

I drop the rock and pull up his jacket, cringing, still worried that he might twist around and grab me. And there it is, in a leather holster threaded through his belt. The gun seems to be made of black plastic, but it looks nothing like a toy.

I don't want to take it. But I know I have to. So that I can shoot *him* if I need to. I remind myself that this is certainly what he was going to do to me.

But what if I miss? Is it loaded? Does it have a safety? With shaking hands, I slide it out. The whole time I half expect his hand to close over my wrist, but he doesn't stir.

It's a lot heavier than I expected. It weighs at least a couple of pounds. I check the sides and the top, but I don't see anything that looks like a safety. I don't really have a pocket that I can put it in. Even though it can't be much above freezing, I'm not wearing a coat, just Nikes and jeans and a chunky red sweater with no pockets. I stick the gun down the back of my waistband and hope I don't end up shooting myself in the butt.

I have to figure out some way to slow him down once he regains consciousness. Because despite how his breathing sounds, sooner or later he will, right? Maybe I can tie him up with his belt. With shaking fingers, I unbuckle his brown belt and start to tug it free. Even as his body rocks back and forth, he stays completely limp. I'm torn between fear that he'll move and fear that he'll stop breathing altogether. Finally, the belt slides free from the last loop. His gun holster falls to the ground.

Nothing changes. His body is still slack. His breathing still hitches. His eyes are still half open. It's only now that I notice where his head landed when he fell. Right on a rock. It's not much bigger than the one I was holding, but it's smeared with blood.

Bitter acid fills my mouth. Did I break his skull? Is he going to die? Did I kill him?

But I had to do what I did. I *had* to.

And if he comes to, I have to make sure he can't kill me. Grunting, I push him onto one side. It takes all my strength. This must be what they mean when they talk about dead weight. In his back pocket, there's the square outline of his wallet. I pull it out and put it in my own back pocket. Then I make a loop out of the belt. One of his hands is pinned under his body and I tug it free. His breathing pauses, but he never stiffens, never even moans. I slide the loop around his wrists, tighten it, and then wind the belt to make a sort of knot. But I don't think it will hold very long if he tries to get loose.

11

I push him onto his back, onto his bound hands, and hope it will at least slow him down a little. I feel something in one of his front pockets, a rectangular shape that has to be a cell phone.

Gingerly, I fish out the phone, and then a set of keys. On the ring is a flat black plastic triangle with two buttons. A fob, the kind that opens a car. I know that much. What I don't is if I know how to drive a car. Or if there is even a car back at the cabin for me to drive.

I have a feeling I'm going to figure things out in a couple of minutes.

I sure hope the answer to both questions is yes.

CHAPTER 4
DAY 1, 5:09 P.M.

I run back to the cabin, following the path and the two faint ruts my heels left. I'm holding the gun. I just hope I can pull the trigger if I have to.

The cabin door is still ajar. I don't hear or see anyone. I step across the sill. It's as cold inside as it is out.

When I take two more steps inside, I see a face. Staring back at me.

I jerk to a stop, my heart leaping in my chest.

It's a girl. Her mouth opens as if to sound the alarm that I am free. That I am alive. When I am supposed to be neither of these things. I scream and raise the gun, holding it with both hands.

The girl facing me does the same.

It's a mirror, of course. A mirror with coat hooks hanging above it. One of them holds a coat that covers most of the frame. I kick through the mess on the floor, push the coat aside, and stare at myself. At me. At who I must be.

Only it's a face I don't recognize.

Snarled blond hair that falls to the shoulders. To *my* shoulders. Fifteen, sixteen, seventeen? Wide blue eyes. Straight nose with a bit of a bump at the bridge. Lips that look swollen. Skin so pale that the freckles on my cheeks stand out like flecks spattered from a paintbrush. Am I always this pale, or is it from shock and blood loss? What I think is the beginning of a bruise shadows my jaw. My heart pounds in my throat and bloody fingertips. I want to throw up.

Instead, I open my lips to look at my teeth. Even and white. I slide my index finger in my mouth and touch the tooth that felt loose before, the bottom left eyetooth. It wiggles. I snatch my hand back, afraid I'll make it fall out. I've already lost so much: my fingernails, my name, my identity. I don't need to lose my tooth, too.

I peek out the red-and-white-checkered curtains next to the front door, then push one aside when I see nothing and nobody. Just an empty dark blue SUV and trees and a muddy road. I tuck the gun in my waistband then take the keys out of my pocket and press the fob. The taillights of the SUV flash, and something inside me loosens. I'll be able to get away.

I've got to get help. Get to safety. Before I go, I take a quick look around for anything useful I can take with me. For any clues as to what happened here, who I am, why someone would want to kill me.

The black stove is unlit. Above it is a stone mantel made

of river rocks, the only place that hasn't been subject to the search-and-destroy mission. The two men must have seen no point in tossing the found objects lined up there: a long, speckled feather; a leaf reduced to a white skeleton; half a sky-blue eggshell that could fit over my pinkie. And in the middle, a framed photo. In it, a man stands with his arms around a woman's shoulders. The woman holds a little boy, a toddler, by the hand. A girl stands next to them, grinning. She holds her hands apart as if she is measuring something.

I am that girl. I look in the mirror again and back down. Even though I think I'm a little older than the girl in the photo, it's clearly me. I have no idea who the rest of them are.

I take the coat off the hook. It's heavy brown canvas with a green plaid lining. I think it's a man's coat, maybe the man in the photo. I put it on, curling my damaged fingers when I push them through the sleeve so they don't touch the cloth. The cuffs hang to just above my fingertips. I slide the photo into one of the coat's front patch pockets.

I quickly check the two small bedrooms. One has a double bed, the other has two sets of bunk beds. The sheets have been yanked off and the mattresses hang half off the bed, slit open. On the floor of each closet, there's a small heap of clothes and hangers, along with a jumble of boots, skis, snowboards, fishing poles, old games, mismatched sheets, and faded blankets. Dresser drawers gape open, but the drawers are nearly empty. I see wool socks, a blue bandanna, a hairbrush with a few blond hairs wound around the bristles. I'm too nervous to keep looking. The back of my neck itches, and I keep jerking my head around, expecting to see the guy I left tied up standing in the doorway.

Only, no one is ever there.

In the bathroom, shampoo, conditioner, and sunscreen have been squirted from their now empty bottles. I get lucky and find a few dry Band-Aids lying next to a mess of ruined ones. I wrap my poor throbbing fingers and let the wrappers fall to the floor. I'm heading toward the door before I've even got the second one all the way bound.

Twenty seconds later I'm sitting in a stranger's car, with a stranger's coat on my back, and with the picture of some more strangers in my pocket.

And then there's the gun on the seat beside me.

I put the key in the ignition, turn the key, and release the emergency brake. All these things happen automatically.

So I guess I know how to do this. I revise my age upward. I'm probably at least sixteen. With my hands slick on the wheel, I turn in a big circle and head for the road.

CHAPTER 5
DAY 1, 5:23 P.M.

I follow a set of graveled tracks pitted with muddy puddles. They wind between tall fir trees, and then suddenly ahead of me is a road. I come to a stop. It's a narrow road with soft shoulders, just big enough for two cars. Not even a white line down the middle. No street signs. Nothing to tell me where I am. Or where to go.

I wait for a few seconds, but no cars pass. There are no streetlights or even telephone poles, and it's only then that I realize it's growing dark. The clock on the dash says 5:23. It must be late fall, or early spring. No signs of old snow, so I'm guessing fall.

Which way should I go? Left or right? The road slopes down from left to right. It feels like I'm up in the mountains someplace. If I turn left and go higher, I could be turning away from civilization.

So I turn right, my damp palms sliding on the wheel.

And realize only after I hear the *tick-tick-tick* that I put on the turn signal first, like there's someone else out here to see.

As I drive down the new road, I look for other cabins, other roads, signs, some evidence of people, of a place I can go to for help, but there's nothing. Just trees pressing up against the edges of the road. The speedometer says I'm going only thirty miles an hour, but I'm afraid to go faster. Are my lights on? I watch the road and see them, two pale cones of light pushing ahead of me. It's definitely getting darker. The sun is sliding down behind the trees on my right. That must mean I'm driving south.

Why do I keep gathering scraps of facts? Like, what difference does it make if it's day or night? Winter or summer? What difference does it make which direction I'm going?

What's important is that I don't know who I am.

And that two men want to kill me.

As I'm going around a bend, a blue Subaru wagon suddenly appears and passes me. It's gone before I can decide what to do. The next time I see a car, should I honk and flash my lights and scream out my window that I'm in trouble? But the person driving the car that passed me was a guy. And I never saw the man who gave the order to finish me off. What if I try to stop someone and it turns out to be the person who ordered my death? What if he's coming back to find out where his friend is?

It's not safe to ask for help out here. Not where there aren't any witnesses. I'll keep driving until I get to a town. And then I'll find the police station. They'll know what to do. They'll know how to help me.

Then I remember the guy's phone in my pocket. I could call 9-1-1 right now!

Without thinking, I slide my hand past my open coat and start to wiggle my fingers into the left pocket of my jeans. Ouch! Tears spring to my eyes, and I yank my poor bloody fingers back as if they just got bitten.

The pain gives me a chance to think. What would I tell the 9-1-1 operator? All I know is that I'm on a road up in the mountains. Period. That isn't enough for them to come find me. Cell towers are probably few and far between out here. And I don't want to sit and wait while they figure out where I am.

Because what if someone else finds me first?

No. I'll just keep driving. I won't stop anyone for help, and I won't try to call anyone.

But that doesn't stop someone from calling me. Or rather, from calling the guy I left tied up in the woods, barely breathing. Because there's a buzz coming from my left hip.

What will the person calling do when the guy doesn't answer? Will they know that something is wrong? Will they find him—and then set out to find me?

I push down on the accelerator.

CHAPTER 6
DAY 1, 5:34 P.M.

The phone finally stops buzzing. My hands hurt from gripping the steering wheel. My teeth chatter even after I figure out how to turn on the heat. Waves of shivers wash over me.

I'm in a nightmare. But I don't need to pinch myself to know that it's all real. My fingers hurt too much for this to be a dream. Who am I? Who are those people in the photo? They looked like a family. Like a mother and a father and a daughter and a son.

And that daughter was me. Is me. If I can find them, they can tell me who I am. Maybe help slide my memories back into place, like putting a DVD in a player.

The road I'm on meets up with another one. Because the other road looks bigger, I turn onto it. I choose left and hope it's the right way.

I think of something else. Who would frame a photo

like the one in my pocket and put it on their mantel? It's not exactly a piece of art, just an off-center snapshot. The only people who would put it on display have to be the people in the picture, or someone related to them. So was that my family's cabin? My grandparents'? It seems likely.

But then shouldn't I have recognized it? Nothing was familiar.

There's something else. If that girl in the photo is me, then where's my family? Are they in trouble, too?

Are they dead?

The whole time I'm thinking, I'm driving. Twice when I have to make a choice about what road to take, I pick the road that looks wider or has more cars. And each time, I look behind me to see if someone else is making the same decisions. But both times the road is clear. Every time I see a car come toward me, something jumps in my chest. Fear and longing. I want to be saved, but I'm so afraid. The wrong choice could kill me.

After I've been driving for about a half hour, the road I'm on is now some kind of highway. Cars pass me every two or three minutes. So I guess I've been making the right decisions.

But all the cars just make me more nervous. I keep looking in my rearview mirror, wondering if someone is following me.

That's what almost gets me in an accident. When a car in front of me turns left, I don't see the blinking yellow turn signal or the red flare of the brake lights until it's almost too late. I slam on my own brakes but I can feel that it's not going to be enough.

I yank the car to the right, a horn blaring behind me, and just manage to squeeze past.

There's a little grocery store up ahead, but it's dark and closed. Still, I pull into the parking lot. I'm shaking so hard I can barely turn the key.

The sound of my ragged breathing fills the space. "Calm down," I say out loud. "You're safe." But I don't feel safe. Who can I turn to? Who can I trust? Every few seconds, another car rushes by, but they are filled with strangers who wouldn't have any more idea than I do about how to help me.

Then I remember something about that guy's phone. It looked like it connected to the Internet. I take it out and swipe my finger over the screen. It lights up. I have to scroll around a little, but then I find the browser, click on it, then type in *googlemaps.com* to see where I am.

I have to zoom out a few times to figure out what state I'm in. Oregon. Does that sound right? Is that where I live? I ask myself questions, but nothing comes back.

According to Google, I'm roughly in the middle of the state, which is basically shaped like a square. The closest dot on the map is called Newberry Ranch. And when I try typing in *Newberry Ranch* and *police*, I get this: "Located just inside the entrance of Oregon's Newberry Ranch, our Security Department provides protection and community support to our residents and guests 24/7." Newberry Ranch sounds like it must be some sort of resort, but it's only two miles away. And protection and support are two of the things I need.

I wait until there aren't any cars coming, and then I put

on my signal and get back on the highway. In another minute, I see the wooden sign for Newberry Ranch. Above the words is a stylized picture of a sun. Definitely a resort, I think as I drive through a darkened golf course on a road that winds back and forth for no reason that I can see. Even though the road is empty, it feels busy, with signs warning about the five-mile-an-hour speed limit and bright yellow speed bumps to make sure you don't ignore the signs. Past the golf course are houses that look like cabins on steroids.

If it weren't for the word SECURITY on the side of the building and the black cop car sitting in front, I never would think this was a police station. It looks like a cheaper prefab cabin.

I've been watching my rearview mirror, so I know no one followed me here. But even so, the space between my shoulder blades itches. Just to be safe, I tuck the gun in the back of my waistband again like some kind of wannabe gangster. Then I get out of the SUV and run for the door.

CHAPTER 7

DAY 1, 6:27 P.M.

When I burst through the door, a middle-aged man wearing a uniform is sitting behind a desk reading *People* magazine. His name tag says OFFICER DILLOW.

"You've got to help me. Someone's trying to kill me." A sob pushes up from my belly as I stagger toward him. I put my hand over my mouth but it still leaks out.

"What?" He puts his coffee down so fast it slops on the magazine. He bounces to his feet, his hand on the butt of his gun. His eyes scan the flat black glass of the windows behind me. "Is he out there?"

"No, I don't think so." My voice gets higher as I think about how horrible it would be if one of those men was. "I don't think I was followed."

His hand doesn't move from his gun, but he looks back at me now. "Followed? From your unit?"

He must think I'm one of the guests. "No. You don't

understand." My words come faster and faster. "I was at a cabin. Someplace back there." I wave my hand behind me, not even sure anymore that I'm pointing in the right direction. "Up in the mountain. About ninety minutes ago, I . . . I . . . I"—I stutter as the horror washes over me again—"I came to. From being unconscious. I was lying on a floor and two men were standing over me. And one of them said that I didn't know anything and told the other one to take me out back and . . . and"—it's hard to repeat this, to repeat how someone gave the order to murder me— "and finish me off. And then he left and the second guy dragged me out to the woods to kill me." Tears are running down my face and into my mouth.

With every word, Officer Dillow's eyes get wider. "Now slow down, honey, slow down. Here, why don't you sit down." He motions at the chair in front of his desk.

But I can't slow down and I can't sit down. "Look what they did to me." I hold out my bandaged hand, which shakes so hard there's no way he can focus on it. "They pulled out my fingernails."

His face pales. "Really?" His brows draw together. "What's your name? Where's your family?"

I swipe my nose, try to get myself under control. "That's the thing. I don't know. Those guys must have hit me on the head or something. I don't remember anything from before I woke up on the floor of that cabin."

"You said one of the men left? What happened to the other one?"

I think of all the things I did, then simplify it to: "When we were out in the woods, I pushed him and he fell

25

and hit his head on a rock. Then I tied him up with his own belt." I remember the gasping sounds he was making, the sounds that weren't really breathing, and push the memory away.

"Okay, so let me get this straight," Officer Dillow says slowly. "You don't know who you are, you don't know where you were before you came here, and all you know is that two men are trying to kill you."

Put that way, it sounds kind of crazy. "Yes. That's right."

"Let me ask you something." He presses his lips together and tilts his head to one side. His coffee-colored eyes bore into me. "Have you had any alcohol or drugs today?"

"What? No. You can give me a Breathalyzer test or whatever it is you do. I'm not drunk or anything." Even as I say the words, I wonder if they're true. Maybe they did give me drugs. Maybe that's why I can't remember.

Officer Dillow leans closer, sniffs. I figure he's trying to smell beer or pot on me. Then he shakes his head and steps back. "Frankly, this is all a little out of my league. Normally I just find lost dogs and tell people to turn down the volume on their parties." He sighs and runs his hand through his short brown hair, leaving furrows. "So you don't know who either of these men are? The ones who wanted to"— Officer Dillow hesitates—"kill you?"

I shake my head. "No. I took the guy's car and I just started driving. But . . . wait a second." With a feeling of relief, I remember the wallet. If Officer Dillow wants proof that the things I'm saying really happened, that the men really existed, I have it. I pull out the wallet and hand it to him. "Here. I got this off the guy who was going to kill me."

Officer Dillow flips it open, and we both look inside. In front is an Oregon driver's license. The name of the guy I left in the woods is Michael Brenner. He's thirty-four years old, five foot nine, and weighs 153 pounds. In the photo on his license, he looks friendly. He doesn't look like a bad person. He doesn't look like someone who would pull out your fingernails and drag you into the forest to shoot you. Officer Dillow thumbs through the rest of the wallet. Brenner has credit cards, gas station cards, and some twenties and fifties.

As he is looking through the wallet, the phone rings. We both jump. Office Dillow excuses himself and goes into an office in the back. After a second, he closes the door. His voice is a low murmur. I should feel safe, being in a security office, but instead, with the darkness pressing up against the windows, I feel like I'm standing in a spotlight. It wouldn't be hard to figure out where I would go. Either the hospital or the cops. And fixing my fingers is nothing compared to saving my life.

When Officer Dillow comes out, his mouth is set in a thin line. "That was my wife, checking in. And then I talked to the Bend police station. I'm going to take you over there. They've got a much bigger cop shop. We're just a security operation. Frankly, we're not set up for this kind of thing. We don't even have holding cells. They'll be able to help you there."

He goes to the window, and we both look out again at the darkness. "In case those guys are out there, I'll go first, unlock the cruiser's back door, and leave it open," he says. "Then you come out fast, keep low, and lie down flat on the back seat. And you'll stay flat all the way to Bend. That way, if anyone is watching who's coming to and leaving Newberry Ranch, they won't know you're with me."

We do as he suggests. His black car has a light bar on top and NEWBERRY RANCH SECURITY written on the side in slanted white letters. A few seconds after he leaves, I bend double, hurry to the car, and crawl onto the back seat. I reach behind me and pull the door closed. It's only then I realize that I am where they put the prisoners. A chest-high barrier of scratched metal runs the length of the car behind the front seats. It's topped with a plate of Plexiglas, like a second windshield that separates me from Officer Dillow. Only the Plexigas doesn't run all the way across. The last section behind the front passenger's seat is made of cross-hatched metal mesh, I guess to allow the officer to talk to the prisoner.

It's weird to be lying in the back of a police car. The seat is vinyl and hard, and I think it smells like pee. Pee and vomit. I remember what Officer Dillow said about loud parties. Maybe the only people who are ever back here are drunks. When was the last time Officer Dillow dealt with a real criminal? I wonder if he's as scared as I am.

I shift around so that the side of my face isn't pressed into the seat. When I do, I feel the gun in my waistband, poking into the small of my back. I should have given it to Officer Dillow. I'll have to give it to the Bend police when we get to the station. That and the guy's car keys and cell phone. Maybe they can use the cell phone to figure out who the other guy is. The one who left. The one who gave the order for me to die.

Officer Dillow still hasn't started the car. I push myself up on one elbow. "Is something wrong?"

He turns and looks at me through the Plexiglas. In the dark, his face is a dim shape, his eyes black holes. He takes a deep breath. "Katie, I know what really happened. I talked to your doctor."

My mind snags on the first word he said. Katie? Is that my name? My lips move as I try it out. *Katie.* But there's no real echo inside me. It falls flat.

Then the rest of what he said catches up with me. "What are you talking about? What doctor?"

He sighs. "You're an inpatient at Sagebrush. You attacked a counselor there—Michael Brenner—and fled in his car." Officer Dillow's not making any sense.

"Sagebrush? What's that?"

"An inpatient mental health program for teens."

Does he mean a mental hospital? "And that's who I'm supposed to be?" I push myself to a sitting position. "A mentally ill teenager?" I make a sound that's kind of like a laugh. "The only thing wrong with me is that two men are trying to kill me."

"They found the place in your room where you've been hiding the pills you spit out." His voice is soft. "Katie, I know you think you know the truth, but you're imagining it. Dr. Nowell explained to me that without your meds you have vivid hallucinations that are more real to you than even reality is." He sighs. "But the truth is that nothing and no one is chasing you."

"What about my hand?" I raise my bandaged fingers.

"Dr. Nowell said you hurt yourself before you left. Michael Brenner was trying to talk to you about your self-injuries, and you attacked him. You pushed him and he fell and hit his head."

I want to pull off the Band-Aids, but I know that even if Officer Dillow sees my mangled fingertips, he'll still believe that I did it to myself. That he won't believe me and my crazy story. And it's true that the story from that doctor—what was his name again? Dr. Nowell?—makes a lot more sense than mine.

Maybe it is even the truth. Maybe the cabin and everything that I remember happening there was a hallucination. How did they track me down so quickly? Or is my version of what happened wrong down to the level of how long I was driving?

I realize Officer Dillow hasn't started the car. "We're not going to Bend, are we?"

"No. I just said that to keep us both safe."

"But why are we out here in the car?"

"It was the only way I could think of to keep you confined until Dr. Nowell gets here. Since I don't have a cell I can put you in." Officer Dillow sounds sad. It's like no one really wants to do bad things to me, but they have to do them anyway. Michael Brenner didn't really want to kill me, but he had his orders. Officer Dillow didn't want to trick me, but Dr. Nowell told him to. "Dr. Nowell told me that because of your mental illness, your paranoia, you would get into the car with me if I told you I was worried about being followed."

I yank the handle. The door doesn't budge. I realize there must be a way to lock it to keep the people in the back—the prisoners—inside.

Officer Dillow's voice fills with sadness. "And, Katie? Dr. Nowell told me that when they found Michael Brenner, he was dead."

CHAPTER 8
DAY 1, 6:49 P.M.

The man in the woods is dead? I remember the slight smile he wore in his driver's license photo. He looked like a nice guy. Was he actually a counselor at Sagebrush? Or is he really the guy who dragged me out into the woods?

No matter who he is, I did this thing. I killed a man named Michael Brenner. Who was either trying to save me or kill me.

Depending on whom you believe.

So, do I believe what this Dr. Nowell told Officer Dillow? Or do I believe my own memories, which go back only a few hours? Did I just hallucinate the cabin and what happened there?

Then I think of something. "I've got proof that what I told you is true," I say, sliding my hand into my coat pocket until it touches the glass of the frame. "I've got a photo of my family that I took from the cabin. That proves I was there."

"A photo?" Some emotion edges Officer Dillow's voice, but it's not surprise. Instead, it sounds like exhaustion. "Katie, when you're in a mental hospital, I'm pretty sure they allow you to have family photos."

I try to imagine that what he's saying is true. To picture a hospital room with white linoleum floors and a single white bed in the middle. To remember the scent of disinfectant, the fluorescent glow of overhead lights. To visualize Michael Brenner, not dragging me through the woods but earnestly talking to me in an office as he hands me a tissue.

Only the pictures I conjure up are fuzzy and flat, unmoving. My body still remembers his hands dragging me through the trees. In my ears, I still hear the sounds of his ragged breathing.

Officer Dillow is right. I don't have any way to prove what I'm saying. The photo could have come from a hospital bedside table as easily as the cabin mantel. The cell phone, the wallet, the keys, the car, and even the coat can be explained away. In Dr. Nowell and Officer Dillow's version of the story, I took them all from a counselor at Sagebrush who was only trying to help me.

Is that who I am? A crazy girl in a mental hospital? So crazy that she killed a man and then made up a story for herself so she wouldn't have to think about the ugly reality?

Would I even know if I was crazy? Maybe that's impossible. But I haven't heard any voices or seen any visions. Don't schizophrenic people hear commands from dogs and TV sets and their own fillings? In the past hour, the only person I've heard talking to me is Officer Dillow, and I think he's probably real.

And then I think of one thing that doesn't fit Dr. Nowell's story. And it's also the thing that will get me out of here. Because I don't want to wait until Dr. Nowell shows up. Whoever he is, I'm pretty sure that what he wants won't be good for me. In my version of the story, he'll probably kill me. In Officer Dillow's version, he'll just lock me up for a long time.

Neither idea sounds like a winner.

I slide my hand behind my back and into the waistband of my jeans.

"Look, I do have something else that I took from the cabin. Something that will prove to you I'm telling the truth."

"What is it, Katie?" Officer Dillow says with a sigh.

I slide over and press the barrel of the gun through the mesh, angling it right at him. "This."

He turns his head and gasps. My eyes have adjusted enough that I can see how he freezes, not moving so much as an eyelash. If I wanted to, I could pull the trigger right now and blow him away.

"I took this gun from Michael Brenner. He was going to shoot me with it. That Dr. Nowell—whoever he is—told you that Michael Brenner was a counselor. So if he was a counselor, why was he carrying a gun?"

"I don't know, Katie." Officer Dillow takes a deep breath. "All I know is that the caller ID showed Sagebrush. But maybe you're right. Maybe this Dr. Nowell wasn't telling me the truth. Or not the whole truth anyway. Look, why don't you put that down and we can talk about things. And I promise to listen."

I think it's likely that Officer Dillow is telling the truth.

At least, the truth as he knows it.

The weird thing is that I almost trust him. But he doesn't trust me. And doesn't believe me.

"I don't want to shoot you," I tell him, trying to sound tough. "But I will if I have to. I need you to unlock my doors and then get out of the car and trade places with me. And if you don't do exactly what I say, I will be forced to shoot you." I wonder if I actually can. If he doesn't let me out, will I really shoot him?

"You're making a mistake, Katie. You need me to help you figure out what's going on. Put the gun down on the seat and I'll help you."

He has no idea how much I want to do what he says. "Just do it," I bark. Or at least I try to bark, but in my own ears my voice sounds whiny. Like I'm a little kid. Like I'm on the edge of tears.

But Officer Dillow does what I say. He unlocks my doors, lets me get out, and leaves the car only when I tell him to. He puts his gun on the ground. Then he gets in the back seat, and I lock him inside. And I pick up his gun and run back to Michael Brenner's SUV and I drive away as fast as I can.

Not knowing where I'm going.

I only know I can't trust anyone.

Maybe not even myself.

CHAPTER 9
DAY 1, 7:02 P.M.

On the way out of Newberry Ranch, I hit the yellow speed bumps so hard that my teeth clack together at each one. I have to get out of here. Dr. Nowell might turn down this road at any second. Or someone out walking a dog could find Officer Dillow locked in the back of his own patrol car and sound the alarm.

I don't realize I'm crying until I hear my shaky breaths punctuated with little indrawn sobs. I feel totally alone. All I know is that I'm in big trouble, and it's just gotten a lot worse. I'm sure Officer Dillow memorized the license plate number on this car. It won't be long until every cop in the county is looking for me. Looking for the girl who killed Michael Brenner.

I think of how his breathing must have dwindled, folded up on itself, and stopped. Does he have a family, like the family in my photo? I remember the contents of his wallet. Gas cards and credit cards but no snapshots, at least not that I saw. I killed another human being. Is it because I hit him in the throat? Because of the rock his head hit?

I tell myself I didn't mean for it to happen. He tried to kill me, and I didn't try to kill him. It was an accident. Right?

Where do I go now? What do I do? Is there any place I can go where people might actually believe me, someplace where they might think twice before turning me over to the man who claims I'm a mental patient? Someplace where they might actually demand some proof? I think back to the map I saw on Google Maps. My choices are Bend, which is about forty minutes to the east, or Portland, which is the nearest big city, a little less than three hours to the northwest. Either way, I could go to the police station or maybe a lawyer. Security Officer Dillow, dressed in his polyester uniform and reading his *People* magazine, believed Dr. Nowell. Or the man who called himself Dr. Nowell. But a lawyer or a real cop might be more suspicious.

I'm shaking, and it's more than just fear. I'm exhausted. My stomach is a hard ball of hunger, and someone is hammering a steel spike into my left eye. There's no way I can drive three hours. Especially not when every cop in the vicinity will soon be looking for me. So Bend it is. When I reach the highway, I go east.

I need to find a place the car will blend in. Something with a big parking lot, like a large grocery store. Maybe I can lie down in the back seat, pull this big coat over me like a blanket, and go to sleep, at least for a few hours. I can't stay any place where security or police might get curious, might run the plates or ask to see my driver's license. If anyone questions me, I'm screwed. I don't have ID, and I'm sure this car will be reported stolen.

Maybe I should get rid of it. But then how will I get any place? How will I get away if someone comes after me? My thoughts run through the same maze over and over again, never finding any answers. And my headache gets worse.

Finally I see the signs for Bend. I get off the highway and drive up and down until I find a crowded shopping mall. I cruise around in the full middle rows until I see a van's reverse lights come on, then I pull in the space they've just left.

All the stores seem familiar—Gap, Victoria's Secret, REI. I know which one sells bras and which one sells backpacks. So why do I know the names of stores and what's inside them but not my own name and what's inside me? Am I crazy? Am I really a killer if I didn't mean to be one? In the dim light, I look down at my shaking hands. How can I know how to drive a car or how to knock a man out and have no idea how to help myself?

The questions echo inside me. My brain feels as empty and painful as my stomach. But my stomach is one thing I might be able to take care of. There's a McDonald's here, and I think that they have a dollar menu. I check all my pockets, but all I have are the photo and Michael Brenner's cell phone and keys. Brenner had plenty of money in his wallet, but I don't have even a crumpled dollar bill, just two guns on the passenger seat.

I open the glovebox. It's as neat as the car, which doesn't

have a single stray receipt or clump of mud marring a floor mat. It holds a tiny first-aid kit, a travel packet of tissues, the manual for the SUV, registration and insurance cards (both for Michael Brenner), sunglasses, a tire pressure gauge, wet wipes, and maps for Oregon, Washington, and Portland.

But no money.

I sit back, defeated. And then I realize the bump my hand is resting on is the console, tucked between the seats. I lift the lid. The console holds a selection of CDs, two pens, and a long row of quarters in a specially shaped plastic holder. I count eleven. Then I count again, hoping for twelve. But I still get eleven. Two items off the dollar menu it is, then.

I decide to hide one gun under the seat. Brenner's, because it's bigger. Dillow's gun goes in my left-hand coat pocket. I slide the first-aid kit into my right-hand coat pocket, next to the photo. After I eat—because now I feel almost nauseated with hunger—I can rebandage my fingers in the bathroom and check out how bad they are. I also take one of the pens. I need to figure out what's happening. Maybe if I write things down, it will help.

Before I get out of the SUV, I turn on the overhead light, angle down the rearview mirror, and look at myself. My face is all shadows and angles, and my eyes look tired and old. *My* eyes. I realize I'm starting to own this face, the one that scared me so bad in the cabin when I thought it belonged to someone else. I flick off the light, then look around the parking lot. I see a couple about my age holding hands, an old man with a walker, a mother pulling a dawdling toddler behind her. I wonder if it's a weekend or a weekday. The lot's not completely full, even though it's not quite eight p.m., according to the clock set in the dash. So a weekday, I think.

I look one more time. No cops, nobody who looks like they're searching, no men by themselves.

I take a deep breath and get out of the car.

CHAPTER 10

DAY 1, 7:56 P.M.

When I walk into McDonald's, a handful of people are seated in the bolted-down swivel chairs. I count one older couple, a guy dressed in a suit, and two parents with a young girl and a baby in a carrier. Even though the girl looks only about nine and the baby's younger than the toddler in the photo, I wonder if that's what my family looks like when we go out to eat. Do we go to McDonald's? When the mom gets up to get more napkins, the girl dangles a tiny stuffed black-and-white zebra above the baby's face. The baby laughs and the girl giggles. Is that the kind of thing I do? Did?

When the dad looks at me with narrowed eyes, I realize I'm staring and turn away. I lean against the counter where you get ketchup and straws and try to figure out what to eat. On the dollar menu, there are a couple of burger-like things—a McDouble and a McChicken. The McDouble looks bigger, so I'll get that. Even though a side salad would probably be healthier, I decide to get a small order of fries with my last full dollar. I wonder what the real me would have gotten. Maybe I'm a vegetarian.

The only cashier has been standing behind the register the whole time, waiting for me. He looks about my age, with short black hair and long sideburns that end near his earlobes. When I walk up, his thick brows pull together, and his brown eyes narrow like he really sees me.

His name tag says TY, and under that is a little ad for a Filet-O-Fish. I'm so hungry that even the tiny photo of a fish sandwich with processed yellow cheese and what looks like mayonnaise glopping out the sides looks good.

"Can I have a McDouble and a small order of fries?" I look down at the quarters in my hand and then back up at him. "And is it possible to get a cup of water?"

When he notices me checking my money, Ty's lips press together. He looks over his shoulder at the cook, a big guy wearing a too-small uniform who's busy lowering some fries in the hot oil. "I'm supposed to charge you for the cup," he says in a low voice, "but let's pretend I forgot, okay?"

I nod. The tears, which weren't very far away, threaten to come back. "Thanks. I appreciate it. I've had a bad day." Which is such an unbelievable understatement that I snort and start to smile.

He gives me a weird look, like *What's wrong with this crazy chick?* then comes back with my burger and fries and an empty cup. At the counter, I grab napkins and pump out four little plastic cups of ketchup and put them on my tray. Then I fill my glass halfway with rattling ice and then to the top with water. It comes out of the same dispenser as the lemonade and looks faintly yellow. Picking up my tray, I find a spot where my back is against the wall and I can watch the doors.

The food smells so good that when I open my mouth for the first bite, I have to suck back drool. And it *is* good. Hot and crunchy and greasy and, above all, salty. And most of it is soft enough that I don't even need to worry about avoiding my loose tooth. I know I should probably eat slowly, but after about ninety seconds, it's all gone and I'm chewing the last hard brown runt of a fry and licking the salt from my fingers. I even circle my index finger around each of the little plastic cups and suck down the last of the ketchup. When I look up, Ty is watching me, his face expressionless.

Well, maybe a few days ago I would have watched me, too. But so many terrible things have happened today that I'm not going to worry about what I look like to some cashier at McDonald's. I rest my chin on my hand, careful not to touch my bandaged fingers, and half turn in my seat so that I won't notice if he keeps watching.

Taking the pen from my pocket, I pull an unused napkin toward me and spread it out. In the middle, I write, "Who am I?" and draw a circle around it. I make another circle and write in the middle, "Is my name really Katie?" and then draw a line that connects it to the first circle. I make more circles that say, "Am I crazy?" "Was the cabin real?" "Where's my family?" "Why do people want to kill me?" and "Who pulled out my fingernails?" Some of the circles connect to others, like the ones about my fingernails and the cabin being real.

I write more and more slowly. All I can think of are questions. I don't have a single answer, and it makes me exhausted trying to think of how I'll ever be able to find out. It's warm inside the McDonald's and my stomach is full of food. Even my headache is easing.

I don't realize I've fallen asleep until Ty touches my arm. I jerk awake so hard that the back of my head slams into the wall. The echo of a sound hangs in the air. I'm pretty sure it came from me and that it was a scream. I've got my hands up in front of my face like I'm trying to stop someone from hitting me. I let them fall back onto my lap.

"Sorry, sorry!" Ty says, looking at the Band-Aids on my fingers. "It's just that we're closing now." He's holding a wide broom with blue bristles. In front of it is a pile of dirt, torn wrappers, and bits of old food.

My face feels tight and red. "Can I just use the bathroom for a second?"

"Um, sure." Ty looks around and I realize we are the only two people left in the restaurant. Even the guy who was cooking fries when I came in seems to have gone. How long have I been sleeping?

On my way to the restrooms, I stop to look out the window. The parking lot is mostly empty now. It's all too easy to pick out Brenner's SUV. I can't stay the night in the parking lot. But where can I go?

After I use the toilet, I splash water on my face. I want to sleep so badly, but even if I find another place to try to hide the car, I don't think I'll ever be safe enough to stop paying attention, to risk falling asleep. I take out the tiny first-aid kit and change the bandages on my poor fingers.

Although they're soaked with blood, I still have to peel them off, sucking in my breath at the sharp pain. My ring finger looks the worst, raw and shiny. Swallowing down a sudden flare of nausea, I squirt the minuscule tube of yellow antibiotic goop on both fingers, then put on new Band-Aids.

I push the door open two inches and stop. Voices.

One I recognize.

"You're sure you haven't seen this girl?" a man says. "Someone thought they saw her coming in here."

I know that voice. I would know it anywhere. The man in the oxblood shoes.

The last time I heard that voice, it was saying, "Take her out back and finish her off."

CHAPTER 11
DAY 1, 9:20 P.M.

Slowly, slowly, slowly I let the restroom door inch closed, careful it doesn't clunk and give me away. There's no place I can run. This bathroom is just a tiled box, with no windows and no exits other than the door. There's no place I can hide. I could lock one of the stall doors and stand on the seat, but that wouldn't fool anyone. I imagine the man in the ox-blood shoes kicking in the door and then shooting me in the chest. If he wanted me dead a few hours ago, how much more does he want it now? Now that I have killed Brenner?

But one thing is different. I have a gun.

I stand with my arms straight out in front of me, my right hand holding the gun, my left hand steadying it. Or trying to steady it. I'm shaking so hard it's a wonder I'm standing up. I can't just let him take me. I'll end up a body in the woods, the way he wanted in the first place.

The door starts to open slowly. *Wait*, I tell myself. *Wait*.

Am I going to shoot him or try to hold him off and get away? I don't know. Either way, I need more than just a hand.

Then a dark head begins to come through the door.

My body makes the decision. *Shoot him!*

My finger is already tightening on the trigger when I realize it's Ty.

His eyes go wide, and he flattens himself against the door. Hands raised, he slides to the floor.

I look past him into the short hall. It's empty. "Sorry! Sorry!" I drop the gun to my side.

We speak at the same time.

"Who the hell *are* you?" he yells.

"Is that man still out there?" I step back so that I can see more of the hall. Still empty, except for a cart with cleaning supplies.

He lets out an angry sigh and lowers his hands. "I told them you were never here and they left. But I'm not sure they believed me. That's why I brought the janitor's cart. So they would think I'm just cleaning up."

"Them? There's more than one guy?"

"There were two."

Two? Like the two men at the cabin? Maybe Brenner's not really dead. Maybe the person who called Dillow was lying. I feel an odd surge of relief. "Was one of them thin and about five foot nine, with blue eyes and short brown hair?"

"What? No. The guy who asked about you had silver hair, and the other guy was bald. The first guy said you just escaped from a mental hospital." Ty looks like he thinks that's a likely possibility.

"That's not true. But I'm not sure what is. I've lost all my memory."

I wait for Ty to say something, but he doesn't.

"I don't even know my own name," I continue. "All I remember is coming to in a cabin a few hours ago. Not a mental hospital. A cabin. And I was on the floor, and the guy who was just talking to you was standing over me telling this other guy to kill me."

Ty's eyes narrow. "To kill you?" he repeats in a flat voice.

"I know it sounds crazy. But I swear it's true." Would I believe Ty if he were telling me the same story? The scary thing is I don't think I would.

"Why would two men want to kill you?"

I must sound like the kind of person who wears a tin-foil hat and carries a dirty plastic baby doll. "I don't know. All I know is that guy was angry, and he said that I didn't know anything. And then he told the other guy to kill me and he left. I didn't even see his face. Just his shoes. But I'll never forget his voice. Then I managed to get away. And I ended up here."

I expect Ty to look even more dubious. Instead he says, "I read what you wrote on your napkin. That's why I lied to them."

I try to remember exactly what I scribbled down. A bunch of questions with no answers.

"Do you think you hit your head?" His eyebrows draw together. "Or someone hit your head?"

"I don't think so." I run one hand over my scalp. "I don't feel any bruises." Gingerly, I touch my lips. "I think someone hit me in the mouth though. It's all cut up inside, and one of my teeth is loose."

Ty starts to push himself to his feet and then stops. "Is it okay if I get up?"

"What? Why?"

He points at the gun, and it's only then that I realize I'm still holding it. At least it's not aiming at him anymore. I slide it into my coat pocket.

Ty gets to his feet, steps closer, and tilts his head to regard me. "Your pupils are the same size. Do you have a headache? Do you feel sick to your stomach or dizzy?"

"I had a headache earlier, but it's not so bad now. The food helped." I take a deep, shaky breath. "You do believe me, don't you?"

"I believe that you *think* you're telling the truth." Ty's voice trails off.

"But it's a crazy story," I fill in for him.

"Yeah. Except I saw the bandages on your fingers. And on the napkin you wrote that someone pulled out your fingernails. Did that really happen?" I'm guessing we're about the same age, but for a second, Ty looks really young.

"When I came to, I saw a chair with ropes." A shudder races over my skin. "And on the table were a pair of bloody pliers and two fingernails. My fingernails." He grimaces. "So, yeah. It really happened. Maybe it's a good thing I don't remember it."

Gently, Ty lifts my wrist and looks at my damaged hand. Only now do I notice the brownish bruises, shaped like fingerprints, circling my wrist. "There's a first-aid kit in the back," he says. "Should I get it?"

"No thanks. I just put on new Band-Aids. My fingers look gross, but at least they're not bleeding anymore. They told this security guy who tried to help me that I pulled my fingernails out by myself."

He shakes his head and lets go of my wrist. "It's hard to believe anyone could do that once. Let alone twice. And anyway, you've got that." With his chin, he indicates the pocket with the gun. "That doesn't seem to fit in with what they were saying. I mean, if you broke out of a mental hospital, where would you get a gun? I don't think they arm the guards at a place like that."

Now I wish I had stayed at the restroom door and eavesdropped on every word. "What else did they say besides Sagebrush? Did they tell you my name?"

"Katie. Like you wrote on your napkin."

"Did they tell you my last name?" It seems like something I could hold on to. Another piece of the puzzle that is me.

"If they did, I don't remember it. I was busy trying to decide if I was going to tell them about you. They did have a photo of you."

"A photo? What did it look like?" I think of my family. "Did it show anybody else?"

"It was kind of grainy. Like it was printed from online or something." Ty raises his arms over his head, fists clenched, and pastes on a grin. "It looked like this. Like you were celebrating a big win."

I want so badly to be that girl again. The girl I used to be. The girl I don't remember. The girl who smiled and had something to celebrate.

My breath is coming a little easier now, but I still feel like a rat in a trap. "Can you do me a favor? There's a dark blue Honda SUV out in the parking lot, like, five rows back and 45 degrees to the left. Can you see if it's still there? And then I'll leave. I promise."

Ty pushes open the door. In a minute, he's back, shaking his head. "It's there. But it won't do you any good. Three guys are going through it—the two who asked about you and another one."

I want to just sit down on the floor and give up. "Then they know I've got to be in one of these stores. Except most of them are probably closed now. They won't stop looking for me. And they're going to find me."

"There's still other places here you could be." He looks up at the ceiling, thinking. "There's something like eight movies showing at the theater complex, and the Ben and Jerry's is still open. And there's a brewpub on the other side that doesn't close until twelve. But yeah, it's not that many places."

"I don't know what to do." I rub my temples. The headache's back, and the food, which tasted so good going down, now threatens to come back up. "The minute I leave this bathroom, they'll see me. Out there in the restaurant it's nothing but windows."

Ty tilts his head, thinking, and then nods. "I have an idea."

CHAPTER 12

DAY 1, 9:36 P.M.

"You really think you can get me out of here without those men noticing?" I ask Ty. "Out of McDonald's or out of the shopping mall?"

His dark eyes look directly into mine. "Both."

I look away. "I don't know." What am I doing dragging the guy who closes McDonald's into my problems? Even with the gun, the chance that I'm going to end up dead must be close to a hundred percent. "It's probably not safe for you to help me. I mean, those men—they really want to kill me. If you get mixed up in this, you could get hurt. Maybe even killed."

Ty hears me say the words, but I can tell he doesn't really believe them. Maybe I wouldn't either if some guy hadn't dragged me out into the woods. He starts speaking as soon as I stop talking.

"Look, the reality is that you need to let me help you.

Or you might as well just walk out that door with your hands up."

I'm so tired. It's almost tempting to do what Ty says, even though he didn't mean it. To walk out there and give myself up. To pretend that if I do, the next stop will be a clean white bed at the Sagebrush Mental Health Center. Instead of a muddy grave in the woods.

Then I remember the pink and white chips that used to be my fingernails. If I give myself up, maybe it will be worse than just a bullet in the head. "Okay. What's your plan?"

Five minutes later, Ty wheels a big brown square garbage can into the restroom. It barely fits through the door. I open the lid. He's put a new black plastic liner in it, but my nostrils flare at the reek of mold and rancid grease that still wafts from it. I lift my leg to climb inside, but the top edge is higher than my waist and too flimsy for me to balance on.

"Here. Let me help you." He clasps his hands and leans down to make a step for me. I put one foot in, then raise the other and swing it over the edge of the can. Nearly losing my balance, I steady myself on his shoulder. I start to put my foot down, but have to turn it sideways when I realize there's only a narrow rectangle at the bottom. The rest of the space is taken up by big indents that must hold the wheels. After I jam my first foot behind the second, the plastic creaking at every move, I crouch down and try to figure out where to put my arms. My mind offers up a memory, not really my own, but of a photograph from the 1950s, people crammed into those phone booths shaped like up-ended glass coffins. My right knee is pushing against my chin, one shoulder is twisted awkwardly. But I'm in.

When Ty closes the lid, it stinks even more and it's hard not to feel like I might smother. He groans when he tries to tip it back on its wheels. "Give me a lever and a place to stand and I can move the world," I think. Or rather, I *remember*. I have a dim memory of a classroom, a blackboard, a teacher reciting those words.

For a minute I forget about the smell and how cramped I am. All I can think about is how two little shards of knowledge—a photo from the 1950s and an old quote from some Greek or Roman philosopher—just got knocked free in my brain. Does that mean I might start remembering more?

We go bumping along. I'm so crammed in that I don't get thrown around too badly, but I can feel my bones aching where bruises will probably show up tomorrow. If there is a tomorrow. A few times the cart drops down over a stair or a curb, and then the sound of the wheels gets deeper and more spread out, and I realize we're outside. He's wheeling me to the spot where they keep the shopping mall's Dumpsters behind red brick walls. Consumers out to buy a bunch of new shiny stuff don't want to be reminded that everything eventually gets used up and tossed aside.

Finally we stop. "Back in a sec," Ty says in a low voice, and then his footsteps move off as he goes to get his car. The plan is for him to drive around the block a few times, making sure he's not followed, and then to take the back entrance into the mall and drive straight into this walled-off area to retrieve me.

But what if someone else comes to get me first? I realize, too late, that the gun is in my pocket, not my hand. I try to twist my hand back to get it, but it's impossible. Another memory comes to me, but this time it's a real memory, it's my memory, it's not something I learned in school or saw on the Internet. In my memory, I am hiding underneath a bed, waiting for someone to find me. Playing hide-and-seek. I don't know who I was playing with or how old I was or even whose house I was in. But I do remember what it felt like to tremble and wait and concentrate on not making a sound. To try to not even breathe.

But back then it was half delicious. Now it's just pure terror. Because the next person who swings that lid back could be the man in the oxblood shoes. The man who ordered my death.

And then I hear something. The hairs prickle on my arms as I concentrate. The sounds become clearer. Footsteps. Coming closer.

CHAPTER 13

DAY 1, 9:49 P.M.

Should I stand up now, grab the gun as I unfold my legs, try to take advantage of the element of surprise? But what if I knock the cart off balance and tumble out? I'm not sure I can even get out of here without someone helping me.

A new sound is layered over the footsteps. My heart hammers in my chest. But then I recognize it. Some guy is humming. And saying an occasional word. "Baby . . . love . . . do that . . ."

I raise my head infinitesimally, lifting the lid. I ignore how it feels wet against my scalp, until I can just see through the tiny crack between it and the can. About twenty feet away, a gangly guy is throwing a stack of cardboard into a large bin. White cords dangle from his ears. I let my head drop.

And feel a jolt of panic shoot down my spine when the lid makes a clunk settling into place. I freeze. Did the guy hear it? I hold my breath. He's not humming or singing anymore. And I haven't heard him walk away. Then I hear his footsteps start up again.

What I can't tell is if he's coming toward me. Okay, I remind myself, he's not one of the bad guys. He's just somebody who works at the mall. If he does figure out that I'm here, I just need to make sure he doesn't say anything. Most especially that he doesn't yell.

A bead of sweat traces down my back. I'm trembling so hard I'm sure he'll see the garbage can shaking. Just when it seems the worst, when it seems that he will surely flip over the lid, his footsteps pass me by.

I haven't stopped shivering when I hear a car driving slowly toward me, the sound of its engine changing as it enters the walled space.

It's either Ty or the bad guys. Because who else would drive in here? And while I know it's probably Ty, I hold my breath again as the engine is turned off, the door opens, footsteps approach. Then Ty's voice says in a low whisper, "Okay. It's me." He flips open the lid. "Hurry."

"Why? Are they still here?" I put my hands on his shoulders and manage to get myself out without knocking over the garbage can. I'm too keyed up to think about how our bodies press together for a second.

"That SUV you drove here is still parked in the lot, but I think someone's keeping an eye on it. And it looks like there are two guys waiting outside the movie theater. One's watching the main entrance; the other, the rear exits." He opens the back door to his car. It's something dark colored and small, with a narrow, deep dent in the front bumper and part of the hood that must match up to a pole someplace.

"Cover yourself up with the blanket. We need to get you away from here."

I do as he says. It's my second time lying down on a back seat today, but at least this time there's no Plexiglas, no doors that won't open. And it doesn't smell like pee or vomit. Instead, the scratchy gray blanket smells like dog.

For a minute, I'm distracted. Do I have a dog? Do I like dogs? Am I allergic to them? I have no idea. I can picture what I think are all the basic breeds and name them—Labs and German shepherds and poodles—but my memory and my knowledge don't go any further than that. It's like there's a door in my mind. I wonder again how the wall got there.

I wonder what's behind it.

"Don't say anything for a second, okay?" Ty says. "I don't want anyone to see me talking." The car turns around, the sound of the motor changing as we enter the parking lot and he heads for the back entrance.

Then Ty swears softly.

"What? What?" I fight the urge to sit up.

"There's a car behind me." His voice sounds funny, and I realize he's trying to talk without moving his lips. "It might be following us."

"Can you see who's inside?"

"Just somebody with short dark hair. I think it's a guy. He's about half a block behind me. I'm going to make some turns and see if he follows me. If he does, I think I can lose him."

It's like we stepped into some TV show about cops or spies. Only we're not cops or spies. We're teenagers.

"Wait a minute, Ty. If you drive too fast or too crazy

and this guy is wondering if I'm in the car, then he'll realize he's right. And those people probably have guns and you don't."

I reach toward my pocket. I have a gun. The thing is, I'm not exactly sure how to use it. I obviously know karate or kung fu or whatever, but I'm not sure I want to also be the kind of person who is an expert on guns. Then I really would belong in a movie about cops or spies.

The car turns left, then a quick right. "Is he still there?" I ask when I can't bear it any longer.

"No." Ty sighs. "He took the first turn but not the second. It must have just been a coincidence."

What am I doing, dragging some perfect stranger into a mess that even I don't understand? "Maybe you should just let me off someplace."

There's an odd note to Ty's voice. "What? Why?" He almost sounds hurt.

"Because those guys want me. I don't know why they want me, but I don't think they're going to stop looking. And I don't think they're going to let anyone get in the way. It's not safe for you to try to help me. I can figure something out." A yawn surprises me in the middle of my last sentence, so the word "out" is stretched and slightly strangled sounding.

"Maybe what I should do is just take you to the cops. It's not like anyone is going to gun you down while you're at the police station."

"Before I went into your McDonald's, I went to Newberry Ranch. They don't have real cops there, just a security guard. When I was talking to him, he got this phone call from someone. And he said the caller ID showed it was from Sagebrush. I know that's not true. But he believed them. He locked me in the back of his car and was going to hold me for them, but I managed to get away. I can't take the chance that the cops here might do the same thing. I mean, the stuff I remember sounds crazy. Why would two men pull some girl's fingernails out in a deserted cabin? And those men *want* people to believe that I'm crazy. So it all fits. But I know I'm not crazy. So you should just let me out before they decide they want to kill you, too."

"Do you have any money?" Ty asks. When I don't say anything, he adds, "You don't, do you? It's not safe for a girl to be out on her own here at night. I've seen what can happen. I'm just saying come back to my place, one of us can spend the night on the couch, then in the morning we'll try to figure something out."

"Won't your parents ask questions?"

"I live on my own now." The words are flat, but I can hear some emotion behind them.

I don't know what to do. I don't know who to trust. So I end up saying, "Okay."

Saying yes to this stranger. I know as much about Ty as I do about myself. More even.

CHAPTER 14
DAY 1, 10:11 P.M.

Suddenly I feel like I'm suffocating, lying on the back seat covered by a blanket.

"I want to sit up," I tell Ty. If I could just see where we were going.

"Hang tight. We're almost there."

He makes a turn, another, slows down as we go over a bump, takes one sharp left, then turns off the motor. "Just stay down for a second. Let me make sure no one followed us." After what seems like a long time but is probably only a minute, he finally says, "Okay, let's go."

When I open the door and get to my feet, spots of white light dance in front of my eyes. I lean against the side of the car for a second. Ty is walking into the dark. What am I doing, following some stranger into a run-down apartment building?

Three stories high, it stretches the length of the block—dozens of units, each with one vinyl-trimmed window overlooking the parking lot, and one sliding glass door leading onto a metal-fenced concrete balcony that serves as a place to park a bike, a barbecue, or a couple of plastic outdoor chairs. Finally, I straighten up and walk to where Ty is fitting his key into a door on the ground floor.

What else am I going to do?

A little kid is crying in the next unit. I think of the little kid in the picture of my family. Did my brother cry all the time? But that doesn't feel right.

Ty pushes open the door. "Hey, James. I hope you're decent!"

I freeze on the threshold. He didn't say anything about living with someone else. But before I can decide what to do, a guy stands up from the couch where he was stretched out watching TV. His straight hair is dyed black and bleached blond on the tips. He pushes it back from where it hangs over one eye, then bends down and gets the clicker to turn off the TV. James is wearing skinny jeans and a tan T-shirt with a silk-screened brown bear standing on its hind legs, arms raised. He looks a few years older than me, but he's about my height and probably skinnier.

"James, this is Katie. She needs a place to sleep tonight, so I said she could crash here, and I'd take the couch."

"Hey." James gives me a nod, and then exchanges a wordless look with Ty.

Just when I want to run back out the door, a little ball of fur explodes around the corner, yapping. Ty scoops it up. "Hey, Spot. Did you miss me?"

"Spot?" I echo. The dog is solid black. I hold out my hand, and Spot licks the back of it.

"Just think of him as one big spot," Ty says. He sets Spot down. The dog puts his paws on my knee and starts sniffing my pant leg. I wonder if he smells the blood. I see James noticing the stains, too, although he pretends not to when I catch him staring.

"I'll heat up some food for you," Ty says and turns right to go into a kitchen with a breakfast nook. The three chairs at the table don't match. I wonder how comfortable the old couch—which is brown and bears only a passing resemblance to leather—will be to sleep on.

"Where'd you meet Ty?" James asks, perching on one of the arms.

"At McDonald's." It seems like a good idea to leave out the part where I pulled a gun on him.

"Do your parents know where you are, Katie?" James raises one eyebrow.

I realize he thinks I'm a runaway. Well, I am, but not like he thinks.

"I'm not sure." My eyes sting. I guess those people in the photo are my parents, but I don't know anything about them. Maybe they really are the kind of parents a girl would run away from. But I don't think so. I wonder where they think I am.

I wonder if they're alive.

James's expression betrays nothing if he sees how my eyes are shining. "Do you need a phone to call them?" He pulls a cell phone from his pocket and offers it to me. "It might be good to let them know where you are."

"That's okay." I wave it off. "Right now, there's not a way for me to get hold of them." His offering the phone makes me think of Brenner's phone. I pull it out and look at the display. The battery's at less than 10 percent. A dead man's phone. And it's almost dead itself. I push the power button until it goes black, then notice James watching me.

From the kitchen, a microwave bings. We both turn at the sound. "Who wants gumbo?" Ty calls out.

"I do," I say, and James echoes me. Remembering the garbage can, I ask Ty if it's okay to wash my hands in the kitchen sink first.

The three of us end up sitting in those mismatched chairs. It's nothing like the food I ate at McDonald's. Compared to it, the food at McDonald's isn't even really food. The gumbo has bell peppers, okra, sausage, chicken, and tomatoes, all of it served over rice.

"This tastes fantastic," I say, sopping up some of the spicy brown sauce with a crusty roll.

Ty shrugs, looking pleased. "It's just leftovers."

"Then I want to eat leftovers the rest of my life." I concentrate on eating while the two of them talk about their day. I figure out that James cuts hair at a salon, and Ty goes to school before he works at McDonald's.

"Like college?" I ask.

"Like high school. I'm a senior." Ty's tone doesn't invite any questions. For example, why someone still in high school is living in an apartment. And with James, who seems to be gay.

So is Ty gay? I think of how he caught his breath when he helped me into the garbage can. I don't think so.

It's hard enough trying to figure out stuff about me, let alone other people. And thinking just makes me tired. I start yawning and can't stop.

"Let me show you where you can sleep," Ty says.

James tips me a wink. "Quick, before she puts her head down on the table."

At the end of a short hall are two bedrooms. Through one half-open door, I see a tangle of clothes on the floor. But the room Ty goes into is as neat as if no one lives there. There are only a few clothes hanging in the closet. The bed is a mattress on the floor with mismatched sheets and a couple of blankets. Next to it is a stack of library books. The chest of drawers is made of gray plastic.

"It's not much, but it's home," he says, hot color climbing his cheeks. He roots around in the chest of drawers—everything inside is neatly folded, which makes it clear just how little there is—and comes up with an oversized green nylon football shirt. "You could sleep in this, if you want." Ty's face gets even redder. "You'll probably want to shower first. I don't have an extra toothbrush, but I guess you could just use your finger and some toothpaste. Oh, and I'll put a clean towel on the counter for you. Do you need anything else?"

I need so much I can't even name it. But Ty has given me what I need most. A feeling of safety, if only for a little while. "No. Thanks. I really appreciate you helping me out."

Even with the bathroom door locked, it's hard to take off my clothes. I already feel vulnerable. It's only in the warm shower that I finally relax a little. My body is marked with bruises and scrapes, all of them new looking, and only a few that I remember getting.

After I dry myself off, I put toothpaste on my index finger and rub it back and forth across my teeth, avoiding the loose tooth. I rinse out my mouth, then look at the girl in the mirror. Her eyes are frightened. What kind of girl am I, that someone would do these things to me?

CHAPTER 15

DAY 1, 10:53 P.M.

When I go back into the hall, I hear Ty and James talking in low voices. I can't make out the words, just the tone, but I know what they're talking about.

Who—or whom—they're talking about.

The tan carpet muffles my footsteps as I edge closer. There's a flapping noise as someone shakes out a blanket.

"You've never brought a girl home before," James says. "And now when you do, you sleep on the couch?"

"It's not like that," Ty says. "She's in trouble."

"Trouble." James makes a sound that's not quite a laugh. "That's just what we need. What kind of trouble?"

"I don't know exactly." Ty hesitates and then says in a rush, "She doesn't remember who she is."

"Are you saying she's got, like, amnesia? Why didn't you take her to the cops or at least a hospital? What if she hit her head or had a stroke or something? Look, this isn't like the stray cat you kept feeding in the parking lot last year until someone ran over it. Or that baby bird you put in the shoebox. Those were only animals, and look how things turned out for them."

"What about Spot? He's doing okay."

"Spot's great," James says. "I love Spot, but this is a person. She needs to be checked out by a real medical professional. Not somebody who's taking an online class about how to be an EMT."

"Her pupils are the same size and track normally." For a second, Ty sounds older. "Her expressions are symmetrical, and she's not slurring her words."

James isn't mollified. "That's an expensive sweater she's wearing. Nobody just threw *her* out on the street. Whoever she is, she must have a family. She belongs with them. You can bet somebody's looking for her. And they might not like that you kept her."

"Somebody *is* looking for her. Right after close, two guys in suits came to the door while she was in the bathroom. They said that Katie had escaped from Sagebrush."

"What?" James's voice rises. "Like, the mental hospital? So you brought some crazy girl home? Did they say what she was in there for?"

"No. Just that she needed her meds." Ty didn't tell me that part, but it's the same thing they told Officer Dillow. "But she says they were lying. That she really escaped from two guys who were talking about killing her."

"Killing her? What, we're in some movie now? The Sagebrush idea sounds a lot more believable. What if she sets fires?" It sounds as if James is pacing, and I pull back a little so he won't catch sight of me. "What if she kills us in the middle of the night?"

"You talked to her. Do you really think she would do either of those things? If she was dangerous, they would have had the cops looking for her, not two guys who look like businessmen. And who didn't offer any ID that said Sagebrush."

"Come on, Ty. Really? So you think they're like some kidnappers slash killers?"

"She obviously believes it. She was shaking so hard. She was scared out of her mind."

"Out of her mind," James echoes.

"All right, all right. Poor choice of words."

"Maybe they did that electroshock therapy and fried her brain, and that's why she can't remember things."

Ty exhales forcefully. "If you had met those guys, you would know why I believe her more than them. They had a bad vibe. They were all buttoned up and serious. But underneath you could tell they were really pissed off."

"Okay, so if you believe her, why not go to the cops?"

"Come on, you know what most of the cops are like around here," Ty says, making me wonder why both of them know this. "Maybe one in ten would listen to her. The other nine would just take these guys at their word and hand her over. They'd just be glad she wasn't their problem anymore."

"So now she has to be *our* problem?"

"Okay, if you don't want her here," Ty asks, "where do you want me to tell her to go? You know what it's like out on the street, especially for a girl."

"I don't know, Ty. I don't know. Then what happens tomorrow? Are you just going to leave her here alone while I'm at work and you're at school? You just trust her not to make off with all our stuff the minute we're gone?"

Amusement colors Ty's voice. "Hey, she can take off with my stuff. It all came from Goodwill."

"Speak for yourself. I live a little higher up the food chain than you. But I am not carting everything I own in to work just to keep it safe from some crazy chick."

A bubble of air expands in my chest. I can't keep hiding in the hall. I step out into the living room, suddenly aware that the jersey ends about mid thigh. Under the jersey I'm wearing panties but no bra. I'm clutching my bundle of clothes in front of me, and the coat hides part of my legs.

The couch has been made up with a blanket and a pillow. James sees me first. His eyes widen. He presses his fingers against his lips and then Ty turns.

Spot makes a beeline for me, but I ignore the scratch of his little paws on the bare skin of my knee. The dog is the only one in this apartment who is a hundred percent happy I'm here.

"Look. I'll just go," I say. "I really appreciate the food and everything, but I should be going." My mouth is dry. I look at both of them. James meets my eyes, but that's about it. Ty manages a little bit of a smile and shakes his head.

"You don't need to go," he says. "Especially when I know you don't have any place else to go. James wasn't there tonight. He didn't talk to those two guys. He didn't see those men watching the movie theater and going through the car you were driving. They want you for some reason. I don't know if it's really to kill you, but I do know that whatever it is, it isn't good."

I want to insist, to walk right out the door. But where will I go? I've got no money. Did Ty lock his car? Maybe I could curl up in the back seat.

I expect him to keep arguing, but it's James who touches my arm. "Why don't you listen to Ty and just go get some sleep. We can figure out what to do in the morning."

I can barely lift my feet as I walk back to Ty's room. I'm past tired, past exhausted. I throw my dirty clothes on the floor. My pants make a clunking sound. Brenner's phone. Maybe we can use it to figure out the truth, I think, as I put my head down on the pillow. It's nice to think "we," even if it's probably not going to last.

A minute later, I'm asleep.

CHAPTER 16

DAY 2, 7:05 A.M.

In my dream, I'm playing with a little boy. I can't see him, just hear his voice. Music is playing in the background, and he's calling out which animal I should dance like. "Dance like an elephant!" he says in his high voice. I bend over and put my arms together and swing them like a trunk. "Dance like a hippo!" I stomp over the hardwood floor, and we're both laughing and laughing.

And then I wake up. This time I really wake up, rather than coming to, the way I did yesterday.

Initially, I recognize absolutely nothing. I sit bolt upright, knocking over a stack of books. And then it all comes back to me. The voice telling Michael Brenner to kill me. The ruts my heels left as I was dragged into the woods. Brenner lying at my feet, his breath hitching. The girl in the mirror who turned out to be me. The people in the photograph who must be my family. Officer Dillow telling me

Brenner was dead. Ty's eyes going wide when he saw the gun. Coming in here last night, falling on Ty's bed, telling myself I wouldn't be able to sleep.

And now it's morning.

At least I still remember yesterday. I may not remember anything more than that, but it's a start. Fourteen or fifteen hours of memory. If I can hold on to it and add more, if I can keep figuring things out about who I am, then maybe I can build a reasonable facsimile of the girl I used to be.

When I reach for my clothes, it's easy to tell that someone has washed them. Someone—and I sure hope it was James instead of Ty—has folded up my bra, sweater, and jeans, and even matched up my socks and made them into a ball. Only my coat is in the same heap where it was yesterday.

A shiver dances across my skin when I realize whoever did it came in here at least twice last night, and I didn't hear a thing. Didn't stir. Good thing I'm safe here.

I get dressed. My jeans are faintly damp, and the left thigh still shows the shadow of a bloodstain.

When I go down the hall, the two of them are sitting at the dining room table with a box of Trix. The bowls in front of them are empty except for colored milk. Ty is just lifting his to his lips when he sees me. He puts it down so fast it sloshes on the table. I hide a smile. It's the first time I remember smiling.

"Hey," he says. "How'd you sleep?"

"I didn't think I would, but I did." I decide not to say thanks for washing my clothes. Too embarrassing.

"And how do you feel?" He's looking at me closely, and I wonder if he's checking my pupils again.

"Kind of achy, but okay. My fingers don't hurt as much."

"Let me take a look at them. If they get infected, you could be in real trouble." Ty gets up, and then for some reason grabs a box of tinfoil from a kitchen drawer.

We end up crowded in the small bathroom—Ty and me over the sink, James in the doorway. Spot is underfoot, and I have to watch where I step. I try to pull off the Band-Aids, but they're stuck. I blink back tears of pain.

"I looked it up," he says. "Bandages will stick until your nail beds have toughened up." He fills the sink with warm water, submerges my hand, and begins to gently tug the Band-Aids free. His own nails are clean, short, and square. Finally, he pulls the last bit of brown-stained bandage loose, and I lift out my hand. My two fingers look oddly naked. The part that should be hidden by the nails is pink skin-colored and only a little puffy. They're not bleeding anymore.

James steps closer and then swears, softly. His upper lip curls. "Who in the hell could do that to somebody else?"

"Whatever they wanted to know," Ty says, "they must have thought it was important." He looks at me. "How bad do they hurt now?"

The water woke them up. "They're pretty tender."

He leans over my hand, gently presses on my ring finger just below where my nail used to start. "The nail sulcuses don't look infected. Or maybe it's sulci. Like octopus—octopi."

"The what?" I ask.

"That groove at the base of the nail is called the nail sulcus. It's where the nail grows out. I was on an emergency medicine site last night. It said your nails should grow back in four or five months."

"He wants to be an EMT," James says.

Ty's face reddens. "I'm taking an online class. After I graduate I'm going to go to Central Oregon Community to get certified." From a drawer, he takes a small tube and squirts some yellowish goo on the bed of each missing nail. Then he tears off a piece of tinfoil and picks up the scissors. "I"m going to make you some artificial nails that won't stick." He uses my good hand as a model for the foil nails. It takes several tries. The silvery pieces need to be a lot smaller than you would think. He slides the edge of each one under a cuticle and then wraps each finger in a thin layer of gauze. He picks up a roll of skin-colored mesh bandage. "I figure this doesn't stand out quite as much as white would."

"Look," James says from the doorway, "I know you guys were having fun yesterday making your big escape and all, but you really need to go to the police. They can protect Katie and figure out what happened."

Maybe James is right. In daylight, yesterday seems crazy.

I nod at the clock on the wall. It's 7:17. "What about school?"

Ty doesn't meet my eyes. "I decided I'm staying home today."

"What will that do to your grades, young man?" James asks. He turns to me. "Somebody's got to play mom around here. And speaking of moms, how do you want your eggs? Over easy or scrambled?"

"Scrambled, please."

"What about you?" He looks at Ty.

"The same." We all head back to the kitchen. As James takes a carton from the refrigerator, I wonder if the eggs are only making an appearance because I'm here. Maybe Trix is really their normal breakfast, and the eggs are a little bit of a show. And what about me? How do I normally begin my days? With scrambled eggs, Trix, or a handful of colored pills doled out by a nurse?

James starts cracking eggs into a white ceramic bowl. "I know you told Ty some of it, but could you maybe start from the top and tell me exactly what happened to you?"

"Sure." Some feeling I can't name twists inside me, like I've swallowed a piece of glass and it's slowly moving through my gut. But I start with waking up on the floor with my fingernails on the table. They ask an occasional question, like whether I ever saw more of the other man than just his shoes. I don't leave out any of it, not even how Michael Brenner hit his head on the rock.

While I'm talking, James finishes the eggs and splits them between Ty and me. He's mixed in some shredded cheddar cheese, and it's *so* good. My tooth doesn't feel as loose as it did yesterday, so I can chew on both sides of my mouth. In between huge bites, I describe how I drove off and met Officer Dillow, the phone call he got, and how I locked him in his own security car and took his gun.

"It sounds like this Dr. Nowell—if that's his real name—used a spoof card," James says.

"What's that?" Ty asks.

"Once you buy the card, you call a special phone

number, enter a PIN, and then you put in the name and number you want to show up on the caller ID. So your guy Nowell could have called from any place in the world, but when this Officer Dillow answered the phone, it would have said Sagebrush Mental Hospital."

"Wait, Katie," Ty says. "Going back to what you said earlier. How do you know this other guy's name? This Brenner?"

I explain about Brenner's wallet, which Officer Dillow took. "I still have his phone though." I push back my empty plate, get the phone from Ty's room, then turn it on. "The battery says it's at seven percent. Do you guys have a charger for this kind of phone?" They look at the bottom and shake their heads.

"Here," Ty says, "let me see what's on it." He starts to hold out his hand, then pulls it back. "Maybe I shouldn't touch it. It's got that guy's fingerprints on it."

"Too late for that. I've already touched it all over." I hand it to him.

He grabs a piece of paper and a pen and starts scrolling back through the phone with one hand and writing down numbers with the other. "I'm making a list of all the numbers he called and that called him." After he's written about eight numbers, he pushes some more buttons, holds the phone up to listen to it, shakes his head, and lowers it. He looks at us. "There's nine messages in the voicemail box, but it wants a password." He presses some more buttons. "Lots of text messages. The most recent one says, 'Call me ASAP.' The one before that says, 'Where are you?' And before that it was, 'Have you taken care of things?' They're all from Nowell."

Nowell, the doctor who works at Sagebrush? Or Nowell, the man who wants to kill me?

The last one was sent about the time I was jumping into Brenner's car. My scalp prickles. "Things" must mean me. From the looks on their faces, James and Ty know it, too.

James pushes his chair back and grabs a silver laptop from the coffee table in the living room. He sits back down next to me. "Let's see who this Michael Brenner is." Ty gets up and stands behind us. James opens the computer, and Yahoo.com loads onto the screen. He starts to type in "Michael Brenner" into the search bar, then turns to me. "Was that B–R–E or B–R–U?"

"Wait," Ty says. "Where did you say that security guy was?"

"Newberry Ranch. It's like a resort."

He points, his finger shaking. "Look at that."

It's the part of the screen that shows national and local headlines. Halfway down, one reads, "Newberry Ranch Security Guard Found Shot to Death in Patrol Car."

CHAPTER 17

DAY 2, 7:50 A.M.

As I stare at the headline, I can't breathe. James clicks. The page opens, and we all lean in closer to read it.

NEWBERRY RANCH SECURITY GUARD FOUND SHOT TO DEATH IN PATROL CAR

Newberry Ranch, Ore. (AP)—A security officer was found dead in his official vehicle at the Newberry Ranch and Resort near Bend, Oregon, late last night. Police are investigating the death as a homicide.

Authorities say that the body of Newberry Ranch security guard Lloyd Dillow was found in his patrol car around 11 p.m. last night. The body was discovered by a person staying at the resort. Dillow, 44, had been shot in the chest. He was pronounced dead at the scene.

His body was taken to the medical examiner's office in Bend for an autopsy, but the death is being considered a homicide.

Authorities questioned nearby residents who reported hearing no signs of a struggle.

A source familiar with the case says that authorities are investigating the possibility of a link between the homicide and a teenage girl who may have been the last person to see him alive. The girl is described as having blond hair and wearing jeans, a red sweater, and a man's brown canvas coat.

Dillow, who had been employed by Newberry Ranch for five years, worked the evening shift alone. "It's just a big loss," said Mel Clark, the head of the Newberry Ranch Residents' Association. "Lloyd was extremely dedicated to his job."

The police are still investigating. Anyone with information related to the shooting is asked to call Crime Stoppers at 541-555-8588.

Two pairs of eyes swivel to me. It's hard to speak. The air feels trapped in my lungs. "Officer Dillow can't be dead." My voice sounds strangled. "I left him locked up in the back seat of his car. He was perfectly fine." I think of how his face paled when I told him about my missing fingernails, how he promised to listen to me even when I was pointing a gun at him. As terrible as it is to think of Brenner's death, I can sort of deal with it because it was an accident and I didn't have a choice. He was going to kill me. But Officer Dillow— all he wanted to do was help me. He just wanted to do what was right.

"You said your memory's gone," James says calmly. "What if you just don't remember what you did to him?"

"No! I remember everything after I woke up on the

floor of that cabin. It's *before* the cabin that I don't remember. Not after."

But how do I know that's true? Maybe my memory still has holes in it. Maybe the reason I don't remember things is because they're bad things. I mean, I don't remember having my fingernails pulled out, and that would obviously be a terrible memory. Maybe I don't remember shooting Officer Dillow because that would be a terrible memory, too.

But with Officer Dillow, I remember everything else that happened—driving to Newberry Ranch, talking to him, the phone call he answered, locking him in the car, driving away, meeting Ty. If I shot him, then the shooting part is the only thing I don't remember. So it's not the same.

Could my mind be playing a different trick on me? Giving me false memories instead of no memory at all? But it's too hard to believe I'm remembering an alternate version of events.

"Why would I shoot him?" I look at Ty as if he really has the answers.

"So you wouldn't have to go back to the mental hospital." He runs his hand through his hair so it stands up like a rooster's comb. "Who else would have a reason for shooting him?"

"Well, someone had a reason for trying to kill me, and I have no idea what that was. And the only reason to believe I was in a mental hospital was that whoever called Officer Dillow said that." I'm thinking out loud now. "And they said they were coming to get me. So *they* must be the ones who did it. Maybe he asked too many questions. So they killed him. And if whoever called about me killed him, it proves that their story isn't true. They must have done it to shut him up." Something occurs to me and I let out a little moan. "Oh."

"What's wrong?" Ty asks.

"I took his gun. He couldn't even defend himself. I took his gun, and now he's dead."

"You couldn't have known that was going to happen." Ty touches my shoulder.

"Too bad all your fingers weren't bandaged," James says. "Or you weren't wearing gloves."

We both turn to look at him.

"Why?" I ask.

"Because your fingerprints have got to be all over that guy's security car."

The few facts I know shift and fall into a different pattern, like twisting a kaleidoscope. "Maybe they didn't kill Officer Dillow for asking questions. Or maybe that wasn't the only reason. Maybe they did it so that they could blame me. I can't go to the cops now. Why would they ever believe me? After all, I really *was* there and I even took his gun."

"Okay," James says. "Back up a little. So you were with this Dillow, and he got a call from someone claiming to work at Sagebrush and saying you were a patient there."

"That's right." I hope he's not going to try to start proving or disproving my mental health.

"But how did they know you were there?"

"Maybe they just started calling all the places nearby where they thought I might go for help." I have the nagging feeling I'm overlooking something.

Ty's eyes go wide. "Then how did they know you were at the mall?"

In my panic last night, I hadn't thought about that. Now the three of us think of the answer at the same time.

"The phone!" I grab Brenner's phone and turn it off. Is that enough? I take out the battery and slip it in one pocket and the phone in the other.

James gets up and goes to the window that looks out over the parking lot. He presses his face up to a gap between the blinds. "Oh crap."

My heart leaps in my chest. "What?"

"Guys in suits. It looks like they're going door to door."

"How many?" Ty asks.

I'm too scared to even speak. They'll find me, and when they do, they're going to kill me.

"Two," James says, then turns his head from side to side. "No, make that three."

"Is there a back door to this apartment?" I already know the answer before Ty shakes his head.

James steps back. "They're knocking on the neighbor's door."

We can hear the raps through the thin walls, then his neighbor's voice. I'm glad we came here late at night, when nobody was outside. When I might have slipped in unnoticed.

But I guess that doesn't matter now. Because in the next couple of minutes someone is going to knock on this door. I look around for a place I can conceal myself. But this place is so small, I already know the answer.

There is no place to hide.

CHAPTER 18
DAY 2, 7:58 A.M.

I run to the back of the apartment and peek through the vinyl blinds. Are men out there, too? The window is mostly covered by a bush, but past that all I can see are tree trunks, bark dust, and more bushes. The ground rises up, so I can't see very far. But no men in suits.

My head filled with panicked thoughts of escape, I reach through the slats and thumb the catch shaped like a half-moon. Then I start to slide the window up. Halfway up, it sticks. And worse than that, I see the fine black mesh of a screen behind it. But I can't see any clips holding it in place or a way to slide it out of the way. The only way to go out it would be to cut it first. And we don't have time.

I hear a soft sound repeated over and over and realize it's me. Whimpering.

There's a knock on the door. James gasps and turns toward us. Ty grabs my wrist. His lips are pulled back from his teeth. The three of us stare at each other wordlessly, then Ty pulls me down the hall toward his room.

"Just a second," James calls out. "I'm coming."

In his room, Ty pushes me toward the closet. I lean down, snatch my coat, then step through the closet door. My ankle turns as I step on one of his shoes. Ty crowds in next to me.

"Who is it?" James calls out.

Softly, softly Ty closes the door. It makes a snicking sound when it catches. His breathing is loud and fast. At least I think it's his. We're crouched underneath the closet rod, facing each other, trapped in this tiny space, breathing the same air, our hearts knocking on our chests.

I'm still clutching the coat. I run my hand down the fabric, looking for the pocket. Looking for the gun.

The murmur of voices is too vague for me to make out individual words. Just a man's low voice, and James's, pitched higher, answering. His voice swoops up and down. He sounds more gay than before. I wonder if he's doing it deliberately—to make them think there would be no reason for him to give a girl shelter.

I find the coat pocket and slip my fingers inside. The solid coolness of the gun is reassuring. I pinch the grip. Slowly, I begin to tug it free. James raises his voice. I still can't make out the words, but I can hear the stress in it.

"No," Ty whispers against my ear. The word is softer than a sigh.

I shake my head. I know what these men are capable of. I can pull the trigger if I have to.

Ty's arms go around me, tight, pinning my arms to my

sides. Just like it did with Michael Brenner, my body automatically wants to fight back, but I repress it. I figure I still
have hold of the gun. I can move fast if I have to. Maybe I'll
have a second or two to catch them by surprise.

Ty's arms relax but don't fall away. His breath tickles my
ear. His body, pressed up against me, is warm and strong.
And so we stay, locked in our one-sided embrace, listening
for the voices to come nearer, straining for the sound of
footsteps on carpet. And I don't know if we use up all the
air in that small space or if it just hits me all at once, but
my knees go weak. I sag forward. Ty's arms tighten again
until he's half holding me up.

"It's okay." His breath is warm against my ear.

I realize I'm crying only when a hot tear runs off my
chin and down my neck. It's most definitely not okay.

Ty presses his lips against my forehead. I turn my head
and lean into him, into his solid warmth.

When the footsteps come for us, we don't hear a thing.

CHAPTER 19

DAY 2, 8:07 A.M.

"It's me," James says softly from just outside the closet.

Ty and I freeze. But when all we hear is silence, it's clear he's alone. Ty loosens his arms, then opens the door and steps out. I wipe my eyes on my sleeve before I leave the cave of the closet.

"So who was it?" Ty whispers. "Cops?"

James shrugs. "He flashed a badge at me but not long enough for me to really look at it. He said that Katie was wanted for questioning in connection with a murder up at Newberry Ranch, and they were asking everyone in the building if they had seen her. When I said I hadn't, he asked if there was anyone else in the apartment. I told him I had two roommates who were asleep."

"Two?" Ty asks.

"If anyone heard you guys, I didn't want them figuring out there's one too many people here. He wanted me to wake you up, but I said I would just ask you later. Then he asked if I minded if he took a look around, and I said I most certainly did. I told him it was police harassment because I'm gay. I said I have the ACLU on speed dial. Then he backed off."

"Did this guy say anything about Sagebrush? About me being mentally ill?"

James shakes his head.

Ty gets so excited he forgets to lower his voice. "So they must have been lying about you being a mental patient." James and I both turn on him with stern faces, and he drops back to a whisper. "They must realize that if they keep telling everyone you're from Sagebrush, then pretty soon someone's going to call Sagebrush. And then they'll learn you were never there at all."

I hope Ty is right. Enough crazy stuff has happened to me already. I don't want to *be* crazy, too. "Then maybe they're lying about what happened to Officer Dillow!" I feel a surge of hope.

They just exchange looks. Finally Ty says, "It would be a lot easier to frame you for murder if they actually had a dead body."

"But who would do something that drastic?" My stomach hurts. "Kill a guy just because he's the first person I ask for help?"

Ty swallows. "They must really be covering up something bad."

"I've got to leave before anything bad happens to you two." I slide one arm into the coat. "I just need to figure out how to get out of here without them noticing."

"You can bet they'll be watching anyone leaving these apartments," James points out.

"I could cut the screen and go through the back window."

James shakes his head. "What? You don't think they've thought of that? I'll guarantee you there's a car parked out where we can't see it, with some guy watching. And the minute you climb through the window, he'll know you're the one they're looking for." He looks me up and down. "And no matter how you leave, they're looking for a blond girl dressed in those clothes you're wearing. Maybe the trick would be to make you the exact opposite."

"What would that be?" Ty asks. "A dark-haired dude?"

I think he's joking, but James says, "Exactly. And fast, before they start double-checking the apartments. See if you can find her some clothes while I take care of her hair."

James pulls off my coat and sets it aside, then leads me into the bathroom and takes a pair of scissors from a drawer. Before I can think whether it's a good idea, he grabs a hank of hair and lops it off, then grabs another. He doesn't do it with any care, and after he takes out the clippers, I see why. While he buzzes over my scalp, I close my eyes. When I open them, I look like some kid too young to grow a beard. In the mirror, I see Ty standing in the doorway, holding a pile of clothes.

"I don't see any cuts or bumps." James runs his hand over what's left of my hair. It looks like fur. "Whatever made you lose your memory, I don't think it was that you got hit on the head."

He means his words to be reassuring, but I wish it were

something simple. Why did my memory go away? And will it ever come back?

"Do you have an old T-shirt of yours that she could wear?" James takes a dye kit from one of a couple dozen jumbled underneath the sink. "This stuff tends to drip, and it isn't exactly gentle on the skin."

Ty sets down the clothes he was holding and digs around in the bathroom's laundry hamper. The yellow T-shirt he finds is fraying at the neck. Since it came from the hamper, he must still wear it. It's clear how poor he is.

I hesitate. "Are you sure?"

Ty waves his hand. "I should have gotten rid of this a long time ago."

As my head pushes through the cloth, I realize it smells like him. The same smell as his pillowcase, or when he put his arms around me in the closet. Sharp and clean, like fresh-cut wood.

James has me put my head under the faucet. It takes only a few seconds to wet what's left of my hair. He pulls on a pair of bright yellow gloves. I close my eyes as he squirts the cold dye onto my head, massages it around, then wipes the extra gunk off my forehead, neck, and ears with an old washcloth.

At the sound of James's voice, I open my eyes. He's looking at his watch. "Okay, even though I'm not sure the color's set, we need to get you out of here. Time to rinse you off." He runs water over my hair until it swirls clean in the white sink.

When I lift my head, I don't recognize myself in the mirror. Just when I was starting to know what I looked like. Under my cap of dark hair, my eyes look huge. I don't look like a girl or a guy. Maybe not even human. I look like some wild animal baby left orphaned in the forest.

The kind of wild animal baby that's going to get eaten.

"You look younger as a boy," Ty says. "Maybe thirteen or so."

"That's good." James strips off the rubber gloves. "They'll be looking for a sixteen-year-old blond girl. Not a thirteen-year-old dark-haired boy."

Ty picks up the clothes again and hands them to me. "Hopefully they'll fit. And I figured you could put the stuff from your coat in the backpack." He doesn't say gun. He doesn't need to.

They leave me alone to get dressed. I want to take a shower, but there's no time. Ty's left me a T-shirt not much newer than the one I take off, a black hoodie, and a pair of Converses. The shoes are so big I don't even try them on. I just put my Nikes back on. I put the things I've collected—the only clues as to who I really am—into the backpack: the framed photo of my family, and Brenner's keys and disassembled cell phone. His gun goes into the waistband of my jeans, with the hoodie pouched over it.

When I walk back out into the living room, the two of them are whispering. They stop when they see me.

"You definitely look like a dude," Ty says.

"Thanks. I think." I look at him and James, my accidental saviors. "In fact, thanks so much for everything, but I'd better be moving on."

"You're not getting rid of me that easily," Ty says.

"You've already done enough for me. If I walk out of

here acting like a thirteen-year-old boy, they won't look at me twice."

Ty touches my shoulder. "They're looking for one girl on her own. We'll just be two guys going to school. And then we can decide what to do."

"I've already put you in too much—"

James, who has been peering through the blinds, interrupts me. "Two guys are going through the parking lot looking at license plates."

"If they figure out Ty works at the mall, they'll come back here." My heart beats in my throat like a trapped bird. "I need to get out of here fast. Do you have a bike I can borrow?"

James shakes his head, his eyes wide.

"Do you know how to ride a skateboard?" Ty asks.

I'm tired of not knowing things. "There were snowboards at the cabin. So I might know how to snowboard. No idea about skateboarding."

"They're actually not that different," Ty says.

I think he's probably lying, but what choice do I have? He gets two skateboards from the hall closet and holds one out to me.

I hesitate. "I still don't think it's safe to come with me."

"And if they figure out where I was working last night, it's probably not safe to stay here," he says. "Let's go someplace and figure out what you should do next and then, if you still want to, we can split up."

I don't want to walk out there by myself. So even though I know in my gut that Ty is wrong, that the worst place to be is by my side, I don't argue. Instead, I start to pull up my hood, but he stops me.

"They might think you're trying to hide something. Just be who you are. A thirteen-year-old dude. And your name is—hm, what sort of sounds like 'Katie'?" He thinks for a moment. "Nate." He turns to James. "Are they still out there?"

James doesn't move his head. "There's the two by your car, one guy knocking on a door, and I think there are a couple more inside apartments."

"Okay," Ty says, turning back to me. "Tuck your hand in your pocket so they don't see the bandages on your fingers. And once we get outside, don't look at them, but don't not look at them either. Just keep moving. We're just a couple of guys going to school. And once we get around the corner, we'll see if you can ride."

"Be careful." James turns, his eyes wide. "And call me."

"Of course," Ty says. And then he opens the door.

CHAPTER 20
DAY 2, 8:40 A.M.

We walk out the door of Ty's apartment. For one second, I let my eyes glance to the left. My gaze slides past the men in the parking lot like I don't care, like they're nothing to me. Just two men in dark suits talking on cell phones, slowly walking down rows of cars. It looks like they're reading off license plate numbers. One of them is behind Ty's car.

Neither of them is familiar, but what do I know? I sense more than see the one by Ty's car turn his head in our direction, but then he looks away.

How long until they figure out that Ty's car belongs to someone who works at the mall? How long until they figure out which unit he lives in?

I concentrate on walking normally. But I can't even think of how to hold my shoulders, move my legs. Maybe I shouldn't even *be* walking like I normally do. How much do they know about me? Have they seen films of me, studied the shape of my face, the way I swing my arms? Any second I expect to hear shouts, running footsteps, even the echoing pop of a gunshot. The skin between my shoulder blades itches.

Ty is talking. At first I think he's doing it as a cover so that we look more like two kids headed to school. Then I realize he's giving me a quick lesson on skateboarding.

"Okay, once we get out on the sidewalk, drop your board and put your left foot on it, right behind the front trucks. The trucks hold the wheels on."

I nod. A bubble expands in my chest, making it hard to breathe. What if the first thing I do is fall down spectacularly?

"And then with your right foot you take a step forward. Just like you're walking." With the skateboard tucked under his left arm, Ty paws the air with his flattened right hand. "It's not like you're pushing the skateboard away from you. It's more like you're one of those guys in Venice. You know, in those narrow boats? In the canals?"

"A gondolier?" The word swims up out of my unseen depths. In my mind's eye, I see a guy wearing a straw hat and a striped shirt, holding a pole and standing up in a boat. Have I ever seen one in real life, or am I just remembering something on TV?

"Right." Ty nods. "When you're skating, it's like you're a gondolier pushing a boat along. You stay in control by making fewer pushes, but you make them stronger—not a bunch of little paddles. Once you're going the speed you want, put your right foot down over the rear trucks. But don't worry about trying to go super fast. Just try to keep your balance. Okay?"

For an answer, I manage a weak smile.

We round the corner. We're out of sight of the parking lot now. The sidewalk ahead of us is, thankfully, empty.

"Ready?" Ty looks at me.

"No." I sigh. "But I don't have much choice, do I?" *Don't act. Be,* a voice whispers again in my head. I'm thirteen-year-old Nate going to school with his best friend Ty.

Right.

I take my bandaged hand out of my pocket, and we both drop our skateboards at the same time. Two seconds later, I'm up with both feet on the board, clacking down the sidewalk. Ty is a couple of yards ahead of me.

Following his lead, I keep my knees and hips soft. A smile spreads across my face. Shifting my weight bends the board slightly to the left—and I go left. This is easy! And we're going downhill, so I can just keep riding. I don't have to push at all.

We're picking up speed when it occurs to me—do I know how to stop?

CHAPTER 21
DAY 2, 8:43 A.M.

A few seconds later, Ty curves around a corner.

I try to follow, but my skateboard is going too fast. I drag my back foot on the ground, but my shoe catches. Suddenly my board is sailing out into the street. I run three out-of-control steps before I fall, skidding forward on my hands and knees. At the clatter of my skateboard, Ty jumps off his board and runs back to me.

"Are you okay?" He helps me to my feet, then turns over my hands to inspect them.

"I think so." My palms are scraped, but my poor nailless fingers aren't any more damaged.

Ty lopes across the empty road, grabs my board, and comes back. "You were doing really well there for a while."

"So do you think I skateboarded in a previous life?"

"Maybe. Or maybe you're a snowboarder like you

thought or just naturally athletic." He watches me intently. "Did being on a board help you remember anything?"

"If it did, it was like a body memory. I don't remember any more about me." We're at least ten blocks from Ty's apartment complex, but I can't help glancing back. "Do you think we should get off the street? Maybe we stick out too much here." The neighborhood is a mix of small businesses and even smaller old houses, interspersed with more apartment complexes.

"There's a little coffee place a couple of blocks from here. Let's go there and figure out what to do next."

"Okay." I'm thankful when Ty starts walking without putting down his board.

A few minutes later, he pushes open the door of a coffee shop tucked in between a 7-Eleven and a dry cleaner. Brightly colored block prints of animals—a llama, an elephant, a cat—hang on the walls. A railed shelf holds dog-eared magazines. Only a single customer is seated at one of the small, round tables, a white-haired woman reading a newspaper.

The girl at the counter looks about twenty. Her long dark hair is pinned up in a messy bun held by a pencil. When she sees Ty, her face breaks into a smile.

"Hey, Audrey. Can we have two sixteen-ounce house coffees?"

"Sure." She looks at me, and I have a feeling she doesn't buy me being a boy. "Who's your friend?"

He turns to me with a smile that doesn't look forced. "This is Nate. He just moved here. And, Nate, this is Audrey."

Not trusting my voice to be low enough, I nod. She

gives me a brusque nod in return, then turns back to Ty. "Aren't you supposed to be in class now?"

He shrugs. "It's just health class. What am I missing? Self-esteem, condoms, no cigs, no drugs, no drinking. I think that about covers it."

"Knowing you, I'm sure you've got all that covered already." She winks, as if to underline that she and Ty are old friends. After pumping coffee into a thick white mug, she hands it to him. There's a one-inch gap at the top. "I left room for cream." She turns to me. "What about you? Do you need room?"

I find I actually know. "Definitely," I say. Audrey narrows her eyes and only then do I realize I'm grinning like an idiot. *I know something about me.* It's only a little detail—that I like coffee only when it's got enough skim milk to be pale brown—but it's the first time I've known something about myself without having to guess.

After we doctor our coffee—Ty also dumps three packets of sugar in his, which officially qualifies it as dessert—I take a seat at a table in the back corner so I can watch both the windows and the door. Ty sits to my left.

"I wish I could figure out what to do next." I rest my cheek against the warmth of the mug.

"Well," Ty says, "what do you want?"

"I want to know who I am." I think of all the things I've heard in the last day. That I'm something to be gotten rid of. That I'm mentally ill. That I'm a killer. "I want to know what happened to me and why I don't remember anything. I want to know what those guys thought I knew. And why they want to kill me. I want to find my family. I want

99

to know what really happened to Officer Dillow. And then I want to figure out how to make everything get back to normal." Thinking of Officer Dillow, I amend it with, "As much as possible."

"Basically, you need information," Ty says, and a lightbulb goes on.

"There must be a library somewhere around here, right? With computers people can use?"

"Yeah there is," Ty says as he pulls out his cell phone and checks the time, "but it won't open for more than an hour." He sees the way I'm staring at his phone. "What?"

"The only way those men could have figured out where I went is because of Brenner's phone. What if they can figure out where we are through your phone? Maybe you should turn it off. And take out the battery."

His mouth twists. "What if James tries to call?"

"You could check your voicemail later from a pay phone."

With a sigh, Ty turns his phone off and slides open the battery compartment.

Another customer has come in, a young woman with a baby in a stroller. Audrey walks around the counter to admire the sleeping infant.

"So how do you know Audrey?"

"I was homeless for a while last summer."

I blink in surprise.

"Audrey was too. Still is." He looks at her and then away, and runs his thumb across his lips. "It's rougher for girls out there. I tried to keep an eye on her. When I moved in with James, I gave her my tent."

Audrey is making the other woman's coffee, laughing.

"She's homeless?"

Ty flicks the underside of his thumbnail against his two front teeth. "How is she supposed to live on minimum wage when she only works twenty hours a week?"

"So she sleeps in a tent?"

"There's a good spot near the bike path. I showed it to her. Most people don't know about it. Sometimes she sleeps on the floor here, although her boss said he would fire her if he found her here again. We'd let her sleep at our place, but she says she doesn't want to be a burden. She has a lot of pride."

"But . . . homeless?" It still seems like such a huge thing.

"It's not all bag ladies. There's lots of kids who get thrown out, or who have to leave, or who think it will be an adventure. The adventure lasts about a day. There are kids who go to my school who live in cars. There are people who brush their teeth and comb their hair in public bathrooms before they go to work pumping gas."

"So . . . how did it happen to you? What happened to your family?"

"It's not important." He looks away. His lips press into a firm line, then he turns back to me and they relax. "Let's talk about your family instead. Didn't you say you had a picture of them?"

I pull the backpack onto my lap and take out the framed photo. "I took this from the cabin. I think this is my family because that's obviously me." I tap my face. "But that's all I know. And it's not like you can tell anything by looking at it. Just four people in a snapshot."

"Wait a minute." Ty points at something in the background. "What's that?"

CHAPTER 22
DAY 2, 9:32 A.M.

Ty's not pointing at anyone in the photo but rather at something behind us.

I haven't really looked at the background until now. But the four people—the two adults who must be my parents, the little kid who I guess is my brother, and the girl I'm beginning to recognize as me—are all standing in front of a brick building. The sign reads MULTNOMAH ACADEMY OF—and then it's cut off by the man's shoulder. My dad's shoulder.

"That must be where I go to school," I say. And it feels as if another piece of the puzzle snicks into place, or nearly does, which I'm starting to think is about as good as it gets.

"Multnomah must mean Multnomah County," Ty says. "Which means Portland."

"So then what am I doing out here in Bend?"

Ty shrugs. "Didn't you say that place where you woke

up looked like a vacation cabin? Maybe your family was out here for a weekend and something went wrong."

Then where's my family? Why was the ransacked cabin empty except for me and the two men? I just nod, tracing my finger over the figures of the mom, the dad, the little boy. Will I ever touch my family in real life? If I had gone deeper into the woods instead of out of them, gone to the place where Michael Brenner was dragging me, would I have found them sprawled on pine needles, with bullet holes between their eyes? If I never remember them and they're already dead—as I am beginning to fear they must be—will it be as if they were never alive?

Ty touches my hand. "I should go back and get my car. Then we could drive over to Portland and see if someone there knows what happened. Maybe your family's even there."

"You can't go back, Ty. It's not safe. If they tracked Brenner's phone to the mall and then to your apartment complex, it won't be long before they figure out that you're the one who has both things in common."

Ty opens his mouth to argue, then closes it when he sees my expression. Despite the men hunting me, despite my missing fingernails, I think this whole thing is still a game to him. Crowding into closets like kids playing hide-and-seek. He never heard Brenner's breath hitching as he lay so still on the ground. He never saw Officer Dillow's face when I pointed the gun at him.

Dillow's gun is now digging into my stomach. At this moment, I might be the only girl in America with a gun in her waistband and a coffee mug cradled in her hands.

Ty takes a last sip and then looks at the clock on the wall. "We could probably leave now and get to the library just as it opens. I'll make sure the street's clear." He gets to his feet and heads toward the door.

I set down my mug. If it isn't, what will I do? I look around. There's a door for the bathroom, but that's about it. No back entrance. Even Audrey must come in the front. My breathing speeds up. I have the gun, but could I really use it?

Before I completely hyperventilate, Ty sticks his head in the door and gives me an all-clear sign. He calls a good-bye to Audrey. I nod at her as I follow him out the door.

It takes about twenty minutes to walk to the library. Thankfully, Ty doesn't suggest we try to skateboard. I watch every car that drives by. Whenever we pass a store window, I look at the reflections to see if anyone is behind us. But all I see are normal people. Men in pickup trucks, women in minivans. A lady jogging with a black Lab. A guy wearing a neon green windbreaker and riding a bike.

The second floor of the library has rows and rows of computers. Ty drags over a second chair so that we can sit together in front of a computer in a far corner.

"First, let's see if we can figure out why you can't remember," Ty says in a low whisper. He puts his fingers on the keyboard. "Then we'll work on what it is you're not remembering."

"Why and what? You forgot the who, when, where, and how." I start out half joking, but by the time I finish my sentence, our task seems impossible.

Ty squeezes my shoulder. "We'll get there. One step at

a time." He turns back to the computer. In the search box, he types in "sudden memory loss." More than 17,000 results. He follows a link to a medical site, skims a few lines, clicks back, selects another link, and then repeats the process, clicking back and forth almost faster than I can follow. Most of the sites are filled with medical jargon.

He pauses on one site. "Your head wasn't bruised or cut. And you said you haven't been having headaches." His voice is low, like he's talking to himself. "But if it's not from a blow to the head, then what is it?"

He clicks on another link that leads to a site about brain tumors. I freeze. *Could that be it?* But Ty is running his finger down the list of symptoms, shaking his head.

He moves on, checking out more links, as I try to keep up, my eyes scanning hundreds of words. I keep getting stuck on symptoms and diagnoses. I'm not running a fever. I'm not sleepy. I'm probably not an end-stage alcoholic.

Then he stops on a page. "Look at this."

In a rare and poorly understood form of amnesia called dissociative fugue, some or all memories of a person's identity become temporarily inaccessible. In the fugue state, which can last several hours or even several years, individuals forget who they are. They don't remember their names or anything about their former lives, nor do they recognize friends or family.

Unlike most forms of amnesia, dissociative fugue has no known physical or medical cause. Rather, it is thought to be precipitated by an emotionally traumatic event, an event so painful the mind seems to shut down and erase everything, like a failed computer hard drive.

During the fugue state, memories that occurred before the event cannot be retrieved. But unlike a computer whose unsaved information is lost forever, most patients suffering from dissociative fugue eventually recover their "lost" memories. Typically this happens just as suddenly as the memories disappeared.

Ty turns to me. "Maybe that's what you have."

It's already clear that something bad happened to me. Whatever it was, it was bad enough to push restart on my brain. Does that mean it has to have been even worse than the things that have happened since? I pulled a gun on Officer Dillow. I left Brenner to die in the quiet woods. But I remember those things.

Ty is still waiting, watching me with his dark eyes. I give a small nod.

"So something bad happened that you had to forget," Ty says. "It must have been them pulling out your fingernails."

I look down at my bandaged hand. I'm glad I can't remember the pliers. But would that have been enough to make me forget everything? Would that have been enough for my mind to build a barrier, walling me off from everything that happened beforehand?

It's like I can feel the wall in my mind. Do I really want to know what's behind it? Is something knocking on the other side? I shiver.

Ty seems to think we've solved one mystery. My fingernails got pulled out and I forgot who I was. But what if it was something worse?

"That's only part of it," I whisper to him. "What kind

of men would pull out a teenage girl's fingernails? What did they think I knew?"

"Let's see if there's any more in the news," Ty says, typing in the web address of a TV station. It's not hard to find the latest version of what happened to Officer Dillow; it's the lead story.

GIRL SOUGHT FOR QUESTIONING IN MURDER OF NEWBERRY RANCH SECURITY GUARD

Newberry Ranch, Ore. (AP) — A 16-year-old girl is being sought in connection with the homicide of a security officer who was found shot to death in his vehicle at the Newberry Ranch and Resort near Bend, Oregon, late last night.

The girl has been identified as Cadence (Cady) Scott of Portland, Oregon. When asked whether Scott was a suspect, a Bend police spokeswoman would only characterize her as a missing person whose safety was in question. "We have reasons to be concerned about her and we want her found," she said.

However, a source says that security camera footage from Newberry Ranch shows Scott standing outside Dillow's security vehicle and pointing a gun at him. The actual shooting itself was not captured, as the security camera pans the area and had already moved past the location. The source said that a gunshot can be heard on the tape.

A motive for the murder has not been established, but it appeared that Dillow may have been attempting to take the teen into custody.

Scott is thought to be a runaway. On Tuesday, she did not show up for classes at Portland's Wilson High. That morning, her parents left a message for their daughter on the school's answering machine. According to another source, the message said they had discovered that she had sold the family's Datsun on Craigslist, and that she shouldn't come home until they had cooled off. The rest of the family has not been seen since. Reportedly, the Scotts' Portland home showed signs of a struggle.

Anyone with information related to the shooting or the whereabouts of any of the Scotts is asked to call Crime Stoppers at 541-555-8588.

I shiver. The library is all blond wood, white walls, and high ceilings. The tall windows let in shafts of sunlight. It's hard to believe we are in such a light-filled place and reading about such dark, dark things.

Below the article is the photo of me that Ty talked about earlier. My raised fists are clenched in triumph, and a grin I don't think I could make anymore splits my face.

I shift my focus until I can see my reflection in the computer monitor. With my dyed, shorn hair, I don't look anything like that girl on the website.

At least I hope I don't. Because this article tells people that I'm probably armed and definitely dangerous.

CHAPTER 23

DAY 2, 10:33 A.M.

Ty turns to me. "Are you okay?" he whispers. Before I answer, I scan the room without turning my head. Most of the computers are now in use. I'm probably the top story on every local news site. How many people are looking at my picture right at this moment? The changes in my hair and clothes suddenly feel like a mistake. Will my androgynous appearance make people stare at me longer, trying to figure out whether I'm a guy or a girl?

I answer Ty's question with a question. "You know I didn't kill him, right?"

He blows air through pursed lips. "Awfully convenient, a camera that panned away at just the right moment."

"What do you mean?" My mind whirls. "Do you think they planned the whole thing in advance?"

"I don't see how they could do that." His brow furrows as he turns it over. "They couldn't have known which way you would drive after you left the cabin. But they had—what?—at least a couple of hours before Dillow's body was found. They must have altered the footage. Taken out the part that showed you running away."

"Why didn't they just add the sound of the gunshot when I was pointing the gun at him?"

"Because it would have needed to be more than just the sound. The gun would have kicked, there would have been a puff of smoke."

I realize Ty is saying these things because he knows. He sees the way I'm looking at him and shrugs. "My mom's boyfriend used to take me out in the forest to shoot handguns. He made fun of me because they scared me."

I'm starting to get an idea about why Ty ended up living on the street.

I look at the article again. "I've spent the last day thinking my name's Katie when it's really"—I lower my voice further—"Cady. Cadence."

"Cadence," Ty repeats softly. "I like it. It's different. I wonder why your parents chose it. Was it because they liked music or poetry or . . ."

Right now, I wouldn't care if they had named me after their favorite brand of paper towels. Just as long as I could find them. "And where are they anyway?" I interrupt him. "This article is hinting I did something to them."

" 'Signs of a struggle' covers a lot of ground."

"None of it any good." My stomach churns.

"If something really bad happened to your family, it seems like they would have found them by now." He pats my hand. "The fact that they weren't there is a good sign."

"Yeah, but if they're not at our house, and they weren't in the cabin, where are they? They're probably dead."

"Don't go there," he says. "Not when you don't have to." His eyes are kind. Kind and sad. He sits back and thinks for a moment. "At least Cady isn't as common as Katie. Let's see if you have a Facebook page." He types in my name. Cadence Scott. There are a half dozen results, but only one with a picture of me.

He clicks.

"I'm female," I joke, looking at the screen. "That's a relief." The profile picture Facebook has is the same one the TV station used. Maybe that's where they got it.

Then Ty scrolls down to look at my timeline. He sucks in his breath. I lean forward to look at my status updates for the past few weeks—my messages to the world.

TUESDAY

Please don't hate me. It was all a mistake. I didn't mean to.

OCTOBER 11

I've made so many mistakes in my excuse for a life that I'm not sure I can make up for them.

OCTOBER 8

I feel buried alive.

OCTOBER 4

Would anybody care if I died?

SEPTEMBER 30

I'm sick of trying.

SEPTEMBER 17

I can't ever make anyone happy!! What's the point of even trying anymore??

SEPTEMBER 2

Nothing to gain, hollow and alone, and the fault is my own.

AUGUST 20

I feel like I'm stuck in a hole and can't dig out.

My stomach rises and presses against the bottom of my throat as I reread the time on the most recent entry. It was posted less than an hour after Officer Dillow was shot.

I must really have done it.

Even if I don't remember doing it.

CHAPTER 24
DAY 2, 10:39 A.M.

My nose burns. The inside of my head fills with liquid, tears ready to fall at a single blink. But crying won't help me.

"I did it," I whisper. "I really did it."

Ty's eyes go wide. "You remember doing it?"

"No. But look at the time I wrote that. That's right after he was shot." I start hitting the top of my head with open hands. "My memory must be all full of holes. Or making up things that aren't true."

He grabs my wrists. "Stop that," he hisses, then lets go when he sees an old woman with hair as brown and fake as a doll's looking at us. "Anything that happens with me you know is true because I was there, too. I was there when the men came to McDonald's last night. I was there when the men came to my apartment this morning. For some reason, people are looking for you. And they were looking for you before that security guard's body was even found."

"What about all those things I put up on Facebook?" I look at my posts again, each one more crazy than the one before. "I sound like I belong in Sagebrush. I sound like the kind of girl who would do something as messed up as pulling out her own fingernails."

But Ty isn't really listening. Instead he's clicking back and forth on my profile. His eyes narrow. "Why do you have so much visible?"

"What do you mean?"

"Look at anybody else's profile. Like, let's find a Katie Scott like I thought your name was." With a few quick clicks, we're on the main page for some girl with pink hair and black plugs in her earlobes. Where my page is filled with stuff, hers just says, "Katie only shares some information publicly. If you know Katie, send her a friend request."

"See," Ty says. "With most people, you have to be friends with them to get access to more than a few things." He clicks the back button to get to my page. "Everything here"—he sweeps his hand past the screen—"anyone can see. There are zero privacy settings."

"Maybe I wanted the world to see." A guy with a bushy black beard looks over at me, and I lower my voice. Right now, the last thing I need to do is attract attention. "Maybe it was like a cry for help."

"Or maybe someone else wanted to make sure it got seen." Ty clicks around. "You don't have any photo albums. Your profile picture is the same one all those men were using. All the music you like, the TV shows you watch— they're the most popular. The most common."

"Maybe it's because I'm average." I sniff back my tears. "Maybe it's because I'm like everyone else."

Ty rolls his eyes. "I may not know you very well, but I'll tell you one thing: You aren't like anyone else."

For a minute, he is quiet, just clicking on my posts, one after another. There are dozens of comments under each one, plus a lot of "like"s. It's hard to imagine that anyone would "like" these sad little sentence fragments that sound nearly suicidal.

It turns out he's not looking at the words in the comments, just the times they were posted. He taps on the screen. "It's the same for all of these. See, this one you supposedly wrote two months ago. But the comments—the comments are all from today. From when your name started being out in the news."

"What are you saying?"

"I'm saying someone went to the trouble to make you look crazy. I'll bet you have a real, normal Facebook page, but someone deleted it or altered it. Then they put up fake posts that make people think you've been having trouble for months. But I think that no matter what date they have on them, they haven't been there long. They might have been able to manipulate the contents of your page, but not the dates on other people's comments." His mouth tightens. "Somebody's trying to frame you."

CHAPTER 25

DAY 2, 10:51 A.M.

"Whatever we do, we need wheels," Ty says. "Once we leave we can't count on being able to outrun the cops and the bad guys on skateboards."

Sitting in this sunlit library, I should feel safe, but instead I feel exposed. Like an animal that wants to crawl into a dark cave. The sad thing is, I can't think of any place that would feel safe.

Ty pulls a ring of keys from his pocket and fingers one. "I still think I could just go back and see if the coast is clear. And if it is, I could grab my car and come back here." He must see the way I'm looking at him. "After making sure I'm not followed, of course."

When I think of him leaving me here alone, it's like there's not enough air in the room. "It's too risky, Ty. Even if you don't see anyone, they still could have put some kind of GPS tracker on your car."

But being followed isn't the thing I'm most afraid of. It's being on my own again, with no one to talk to, no one to help me think things through, no one to calm me down. Standing in that trashed cabin or driving on those darkened roads—everything was so much worse when it was just me. Under the table, I grab Ty's wrist, making his keys jangle. "Besides, what if you went back there and they kidnapped you or even killed you? These people won't stop at anything."

What if Ty leaves and I never see him again? I need him so much. I have to look away from his dark eyes before I find the strength to say the right thing. "But I really think you should take off, Ty. It may not be safe to go back to your apartment, but it's definitely not safe to keep hanging out with me. You should go to a friend's place and hang out for a day or two." This guy whom I've known less than twenty-four hours might be murdered because of me.

"Look, Cady." He touches my chin, turning my face until I'm looking directly into his eyes. "You're not getting rid of me that easy. So what do *you* think we should do?"

I go with my gut. Without memories, that's about all I have left. "I think I should get back to Portland. That's where I live. And that's where my family is, or at least where they were. If I can find them, maybe they'll know more about what's going on. And even if I can't, there's still the house. My house," I correct myself, even though I have no memory of it. "There was nothing in that cabin. But maybe at my house we can find some clue."

Since Ty's car is out of the picture, there aren't a lot of

options. He suggests hitchhiking, but I have too many mental images—which I think come from movies or maybe a twist on what happened with Officer Dillow—of being trapped in a car with door handles that don't work and a crazy killer at the wheel. Or in this case, one of the men hunting me down. If we stand by the side of the road with our thumbs out, we might as well be lambs hitchhiking to the slaughterhouse.

Which leaves Greyhound. The bus station is two miles away. Ty has us take the road that parallels the main road. It's not super busy, so we're not being eyed by every passing motorist. But it's not empty either, so we don't stick out—just two kids walking around in the middle of a school day.

The air is crisp and cold, but we're walking fast enough that I stay warm in just a hoodie. We're heading toward a tall, rounded bump that sits in the middle of otherwise flat Bend. It's not a mountain, but way bigger than a hill. "What is that?" I ask Ty. It's covered with gray-green juniper and sage, and I would guess it's about five hundred feet tall. A steady stream of walkers and runners are making their way up and down the trail that spirals around it.

"An old cinder cone," Ty says. "From a volcano vent. There's a viewpoint at the top. You can see for miles."

"Sounds cool." It also sounds vaguely familiar, and I wonder if my parents ever hiked with us up the steep flanks, ever talked about volcanoes.

"Actually, they don't think the Newberry volcano that made that cinder cone is dead," Ty says. "Just sleeping. But someday it might wake up."

I imagine all those walkers suddenly finding themselves covered with red cinders and ash, the fiery lava rushing inexorably toward them as they wonder what in the hell just happened.

I can totally relate.

CHAPTER 26
DAY 2, 11:34 A.M.

It turns out that in order to get to the bus station, we have to walk right past a sign directing drivers to the Bend police department, just a few blocks away. Looking at it, I reconsider. Maybe we could walk in, go up to the counter, and explain that while it's true I am the girl on the Newberry Ranch tape, I did not actually shoot Officer Dillow.

But what are the chances they'll believe me? Even in the best-case scenario I'll be immediately separated from Ty and locked up, at least for a while. Maybe forever. After all, I don't have any proof that I didn't kill poor Dillow, except for my own memory. And pretty soon I'd have to reveal just how unreliable that memory is.

And if I go to the police, how will I be able to figure out what's going on? If I tell them my story about mysterious men who want to kill me, it seems quite possible I'll really end up at a place like Sagebrush. So when Ty looks at the sign, and then at me with a raised eyebrow, I just shake my head.

Greyhound doesn't have an actual bus station in Bend. Instead you're supposed to buy your tickets and wait inside a bowling alley called Lava Lanes. The long pinkish building is styled like fake adobe and is set at the back of a parking lot. The parking lot borders a busy street, and on the opposite side of the street there's a chain-link fence and then a sidewalk. That's where Ty and I wait, pretending to skateboard while we try to figure out if it's safe to cross the street and go inside. After all, if we figured out there's not many ways for us to get out of Bend, the bad guys have figured that out, too. Probably faster than we did.

Ty does a kick flip, the board spinning in the air. My eyes flick from his board to his face scrunched in concentration to the parking lot. Little kids, each of them carrying a present, are arriving for what must be a birthday party. A mom carries a long pink cake, a man is trailed by a bobbing bouquet of silver foil balloons. It looks peaceful and innocent, all part of a world where girls would never get dragged into the woods.

And I want to be part of that world so much that it actually hurts when Ty says, "There. That blue Lexus two rows back from the door and on the left. The driver's been there for at least fifteen minutes."

"He could be, like, a divorced dad, waiting to trade custody of his kid," I say, wishing it were true.

Ty takes a baseball cap out of his jacket pocket, pulls it low.

"I'll go check it out."

"No. Don't leave me." I clutch his arm, then drop it when I realize that thirteen-year-old skateboarding Nate would never do that. *Don't act. Be.* I lost sight of that, and if anyone is watching us, it showed. "It's not worth taking the risk to be sure. There has to be another way we can get to Portland. Does James have a car we could borrow?"

"No." Ty shakes his head. "When he needs a car, he uses mine."

Every way out turns into a dead end. I pick up my skateboard. "Come on, let's get out of here before that guy notices us." We walk back to the less busy street, but when we get there, we stop. We have no place to go. Standing still, I realize how cold it is.

"Maybe I *should* just go to the police," I say. But my voice breaks in the middle.

"You still think the answers are in Portland?" Ty asks.

"Yeah." My breath shakes. "But what difference does it make if I can't get there?"

"I might know a way. It's a little risky, but what have we got to lose?"

In Ty's case, a lot. After he tells me his plan, he won't listen when I try to argue. He could get in a lot of trouble with the cops, not to mention the bad guys. But at every objection, he just shakes his head. And finally I give in. I'm not sure it will work, and it's going to mean a bad day for someone else, but I certainly don't have any better ideas. And after all the crazy things I've done in the last two days, his plan almost makes sense.

At the Dollar Store, Ty buys two ugly pairs of men's mesh track pants, one for me and one for him. Back at the library, we go into the men's bathroom—me a little nervously, but it's empty—wearing jeans and come out wearing track pants. No one looks at us twice. As we walk outside, we stuff our jeans into my backpack, which already holds the framed photo and the gun.

Our next stop is Bend's Fast Fitness. The floor-to-ceiling windows facing the street show rows of ellipticals, bikes, and stairclimbers. But there are no windows in the back, which overlooks a nearly full parking lot. After making sure no one is watching, we hide our skateboards and the backpack under a bush. Ty's worried about losing the skateboards, especially the one that belongs to James. Me? I don't like letting the framed picture of my family out of my sight. That and Dillow's gun.

We go back around the corner and inside, where Ty approaches the front desk. He's still wearing his baseball cap and I've got my hoodie pulled up. I can't see any cameras, but we don't want to take any chances.

"Two day passes, please." He pays six bucks cash. I know he doesn't have much left. We decided it was better to have no money than to leave a trail with an ATM card, so he paid cash for our ugly pants, too.

The workout room has the cardio equipment we saw from outside, plus free weights and a dozen weight machines. A large, wooden honeycomb of open cubbies stands against the far wall. Most of the squares are filled: a jacket in one, a water bottle in another, a sweater and two magazines in the next. From here, it's hard to tell if any cubby also has a set of keys. But we only need one.

"Once we get inside," Ty had told me, "I'll need you to

cause a scene. Something that will get everyone in the gym looking at you for at least thirty seconds."

At first, I considered faking a seizure, but someone might have called 9-1-1. So we came up with Plan B. I go over to the free weights, pick up some ten-pounders, and start doing biceps curls. I cut my eyes sideways at Ty, who's next to the cubbies. He nods.

I let one of the weights slide from my fingers. The idea was to just miss and fake it, but instead it glances off my little toe.

I scream. "Ow!" *Don't act. Be.* I take all the fear and pain I've felt in the last twenty-four hours and channel it until I can't tell where the past leaves off and the present begins. "Ow!" I stretch it out until it's practically a yodel. Every eye is on me. Even the people on the treadmills watching TV, and the people climbing to nowhere with white earbuds sunk into their ears—even they have turned to watch. I'm hopping around on one foot, yelling, "I think it's broken! It hurts so bad!" The tears that run down my face are real. As I'm hopping around, I bump into another man doing biceps curls, throwing him off balance. Swearing, he staggers backward.

Out of the corner of my eye, I see Ty pushing open the door in the back.

"I'm a doctor," a woman in a pink tracksuit says as she hurries up to me. She has a long, horsey face and kind eyes. "Let me see."

I hadn't planned on this. I snap back to me, to the real me who doesn't have a broken toe. "I think I'm okay."

"Just take off your shoe and sock and let me see. You could have a crush injury."

Better do it fast and get it over with. I sit down on a weight bench and pull off my sock and shoe. Around me, people are rolling their eyes at each other.

Her hands are cool on my foot. She presses and prods my little toe, which is tender, but certainly not scream-worthy. "If it's a fracture, it's a minor one. We don't normally cast the metatarsals anyway. You should put ice on it and then rest. If it still hurts tomorrow or if it really swells, ask your parents to take you for an X-ray." She lifts her head to look at me, at my black hair as short as fur and the faint traces of bruises on my jaw, and her brow creases. "Are you okay?"

A male attendant bustles over with a plastic bag of ice. "Do you need me to call your parents?"

What I need is to get out of here.

I grab the bag of ice. "It's already feeling better." As I pull on my sock and shoe, I turn to the doctor, wishing I could tell her everything. Wishing an adult could be in charge. "Thank you." And then I leave as fast as I can.

Once I'm outside the building, I hurry around the corner, limping a little. Ty is walking fast between two rows of cars. The backpack is slung over one shoulder and the boards are under his arm. In his right hand, he holds a black plastic triangle, car keys dangling underneath. He's clicking the buttons on the fob. And then he's answered by a flash of taillights. It's a maroon Subaru Outback station wagon.

"Quick! Get in," he says as he yanks open the driver's-side door handle. "Let's get out of here before somebody realizes their keys are missing."

I open the passenger door and lean in. In the back there's a dark blue car seat, empty except for a green juice box and a stuffed Paddington Bear wearing a yellow slicker and rain hat. Ty tosses the backpack and skateboards next to the car seat.

"Maybe we shouldn't." We're really going to screw up someone's life.

Ty is already starting the car. "We have to."

A man dressed in a suit, a gym bag over his shoulder, rounds the corner. When he sees us, his mouth falls open and he just stands there for a second. Then he breaks into a run.

I jump inside and Ty throws the car into reverse.

CHAPTER 27
DAY 2, 1:14 P.M.

We accelerate past the Subaru's owner. His fist bangs on the side of the car, but then he's gone and Ty is taking a corner so fast I have to brace myself against the dash.

It's way too late, but now I definitely wish we had found another way.

"See if you can squeeze between the seats and get down in the back," Ty says, never taking his eyes off the road. He accelerates around a red pickup.

"Why?" But even as I ask the question, I'm already trying to wiggle into the back seat. I turn sideways, but it's such a tight squeeze between the front seats and then around the car seat that my track pants nearly get left behind. Finally I make it, banging my hip on the car seat in the process. One more bruise to add to the collection. I plop into the space behind the passenger seat.

"They're looking for two people, not one. And by 'they,'

I mean both the bad guys and that guy whose car we just stole." Ty's head keeps turning as he scans the road behind and before us, threading between cars. But he's slowed down so that he's going close to the speed of traffic, probably worried that someone on a cell phone will call 9-1-1 about a speeding car. "We just got lucky this is a Subaru. Unofficial state car of Oregon. We'll blend right in."

In order to lie down, I need to move the car seat, which is attached with complicated hooks and latches. But there's no thought required—my fingers automatically know what to press and pull to get it loose.

It must be because of the little boy in the photo. My brother. My brother who I don't remember with my stupid brain, but whose presence is still somehow encoded in my body's memory. Just like driving a car, the memory of how to unhook a car seat has been there all along, tucked away until I need to use it. Will my brain ever decide to give me back any really useful information? I squeeze the car seat over the back seat and into the cargo hold, then follow it with the skateboards and backpack. I curl up on my side with my feet behind Ty.

From this angle, I can see his profile as well as his eyes in the rearview mirror. He's concentrating so hard on getting us out of here that he doesn't notice me watching him. To keep my mind off my fear that we're about to get caught, I take inventory of this guy I've known less than a day.

Full lips, right now pressed together.

Under thick black eyebrows, eyes that are never still, flicking from the rearview mirror to the side-view mirrors and then to the road again.

Dark hair so thick it stands up, except for a piece that falls across his high forehead.

A blunt-tipped nose that makes him look a bit unfinished, as if someone forgot to give it the sharp edges it needs to match his high cheekbones and the precision of his long sideburns.

Basically, Ty's beautiful in a way that only a guy could be.

"We're out of Bend and on the highway now," he announces, and I can see his shoulders relax a bit. "Ladies and gentlemen, the captain has turned on the fasten seat belt sign. If you haven't already done so, you need to stow your carry-on luggage underneath the seat in front of you or in an overhead bin. Please take your seat, fasten your seat belt, and make sure your seatback and folding tray are in their full upright position."

His recitation is flawless, as if he has said it a million times. "You sound awfully official," I say. "Do you moonlight as a stewardess?"

"After my parents separated, I used to fly to Colorado a lot to visit my dad." The turn signal begins to *tink-tink-tink*. Ty checks over his shoulder, and then I feel the car move to the left. We pass a triple trailer. The driver, a big guy with an even bigger beard, smiles down at me. I can't help but smile back. It feels a little rusty.

"So your parents are divorced?"

He sucks in his lips and is quiet for a long moment. So long I don't know if he's going to answer me. Finally he says, "I don't know. What do you call it when one of them's dead?"

The smile falls from my face and I reach forward to touch his arm. "What happened?"

"A couple of years ago my mom decided she didn't want to be with my dad. Actually, she was seeing the guy she worked for. But she didn't say that at first. Just that she had gotten married too young and that she was tired of not having any money. My dad moved to Colorado because he loves—loved—to ski. He also made furniture by hand. People started collecting it. He was actually making good money at the end, which was ironic. Then one day he was skiing off trail and fell into a tree well." Ty takes a shaky breath. "And he suffocated."

"A tree well?"

"You know how evergreens have low branches? Those branches can stop snow from filling in at the base of a tree. So there's all this loose snow and it's like quicksand. You fall into it and you can't get out. Basically, you drown in snow." His knuckles are white on the steering wheel.

"I'm so sorry." I've been worrying about how my parents might be dead. But Ty's dad is really dead, and Ty's never going to see him again. At least I don't know for sure. Not knowing feels like a curse, but maybe it's really a blessing. "How long ago did that happen?"

"Almost a year. And after that, things with my mom started going south. She married her boss but I don't get along with him. Then one day I borrowed his car without asking, his brand-new BMW, and went too fast around a curve. I wrecked it."

I'm starting to understand why Ty lives with a roommate and sleeps on a mattress on the floor. "So you ran away?"

"Actually, they kicked me out."

Something inside of me recoils. I don't know anything

more about my parents than what I saw in that photo, but somehow I know that I'm theirs forever. No matter what.

Ty sighs. "So I was on the street for a few months over the summer. I had a tent that I pitched in the woods. The cops don't like you to be too near downtown. They said we scared away the tourists. That's the same reason they didn't like to see us picking through the garbage at Starbucks. Hey, we had to eat. Then I met James and he was looking for a roommate, and one of my dad's old friends gave me this car, and I got a job at McDonald's and everything started coming back together."

The mention of McDonald's reminds me. "Are you supposed to work tonight?"

"I called in sick this morning." For a second, his eyes meet mine in the mirror.

Ty wouldn't be doing any of this—missing school, missing work, stealing cars—if he hadn't met me. I'm the very definition of a bad influence. "Why are you doing all this for me?" If Ty thought helping me entitled him to something, he would have tried to crawl into bed with me last night, instead of sleeping on the couch.

"When I saw you in McDonald's counting your money, I guessed you were in some kind of trouble. And when I was out on the street, some people helped me. People like James and Audrey. If they hadn't, who knows what would have happened." He looks over his shoulder at me. "Now, would I have tried to help you if I had known how bad it was going to get?" He lets the question hang in the air before saying, "I guess we'll never know." And then he half turns again to give me a smile.

"The problem is, nobody knows what's going on," I say with a yawn that goes on so long I get dizzy. "Not even me. Especially not me."

I should be planning what we're going to do once we get to Portland, but instead my eyes keep closing for longer and longer stretches. And eventually the hum of the car lulls me to sleep.

In my dream, I'm outside the bowling alley again, watching the kids walking toward the door carrying brightly wrapped presents. Only this time I'm much closer, so close I'm walking right behind the dad carrying the silver balloons.

The man in the blue Lexus catches sight of me. He jumps out of his car with a gun in his hand.

And I'm screaming and trying to push the kids inside to safety, but one little boy falls. I pick him up by his arm, too rough, but there's no time to worry about that. I just have to get him inside before he's killed. The little boy is crying and he's twisted around to look up at me. And he has the same face as the boy in the photo.

"Cady!" he says. "Cady!"

I wake up with a jolt. It's Ty. He's calling my name.

And his voice is full of panic.

CHAPTER 28

DAY 2, 3:44 P.M.

"Cady, Cady!"

I lift myself up on one elbow. "Wha–?" At first, I don't know where I am. But for a second, I feel like I know *who* I am.

Only for a second. Then it slides away.

Ty has turned the radio all the way up. He has to half yell to be heard over it. "They're talking about you. It sounded bad."

Bad? I don't have time to ask. On the radio, chimes sound, marking the beginning of the news. "Good afternoon, everyone. I'm Susan McCallister. Thanks for tuning in to KNWS. And here's our top story: This morning, firefighters responded to a cabin fire forty miles north of Bend in the Deschutes National Forest. Authorities say that the vacation cabin belonged to the family of Cady Scott, the Portland teen being sought for questioning in connection with the death of Newberry Ranch security officer Lloyd Dillow. Fire incident commander Rick Ochoa told us that it took nearly fifty firefighters from several responding agencies to put out the fire."

A man says, "The ranger district's initial attack crew was first on scene. They found the structure fully involved in flames, with little chance of being saved. But thanks to the crew's quick action, we were able to contain this fire and keep it from spreading to the surrounding forest."

The newscaster says, "Ochoa would not comment on reports that human remains were found in the ashes."

I freeze. Human remains?

"Keith Pilligan in Portland has more about the growing mystery surrounding Cady Scott. Keith?"

Bitter bile rises in my throat. Is this the reason I can't remember? Was the shock that caused my fugue state seeing my family die?

"Good afternoon, Susan. Where is the Scott family? Police say their Portland home shows signs of a struggle. The family's car, a dark green Forester, is missing, and neighbors say they haven't seen the Scotts for several days. Friends fear the worst. Coworkers at Z-Biotech, where Patrick and Janie Scott have been employed for seventeen years as microbiologists, say the Scotts haven't been to work since Monday, the day before Lloyd Dillow was murdered. Three-year-old Max Scott, who normally attends an on-site day care at his parents' workplace, is also missing. Monday is also the last day that sixteen-year-old Cady Scott last attended classes at Portland's Wilson High. Employees at Z-Biotech told KNWS the older Scotts have recently spoken about tensions at home, saying that Cadence—or Cady, as she is known to her friends—had begun stealing from them and using drugs and even selling."

Drugs? I feel like I'm being whipsawed. Could it be true? Should I feel guilty for something I don't know I did?

But even if I am a drug addict, it doesn't explain a lot of things. Like what about the men? The men who pulled out my fingernails, the men who wanted to kill me, the men who were searching for me—where do they fit in? If I really have been selling drugs, have I somehow gotten on somebody's very bad side?

While I'm thinking, the reporter is still talking.

"Police, however, have still not identified Cady Scott as a suspect in the shooting of Lloyd Dillow or in the disappearance of her family. They will say only that she is a person of interest." From the tone of the reporter's voice, it's clear he thinks it's only a matter of time until I'm charged.

The woman newscaster says, "But there is one person who does believe in Cady Scott's innocence, right, Keith?"

"That's right, Susan. I'm at the Portland hotel where Elizabeth Quinn, Cady Scott's aunt, has been speaking to reporters about her niece. She flew into Portland as soon as she heard about her missing family members."

Elizabeth Quinn? I've just been given one more piece of the puzzle of who I am. Thinking of the human remains, I wonder bleakly if it's possible she's now the only living relative I have.

"I am certain Cady didn't do it," a woman says emphatically. "I've known her since she was a baby. She sends me little notes on email all the time. She's a sweet, quiet girl. There's no way she could be mixed up in something bad. There's either been a terrible accident or some kind of mistake. And I'm not going to leave Portland until I find out what really happened."

The male reporter cuts in. "And that's what everyone would like to know. What happened to Cady Scott and her family? This is Keith Pilligan, reporting to you live from the Winchester Hotel. Back to you, Susan."

The newscaster says, "Cady Scott is sixteen years old, five foot seven, and about one hundred twenty-five pounds. She has shoulder-length dark blond hair and blue eyes. You can see a picture of her on our website." She takes a breath and then says, "In other news around the region . . ."

Ty snaps off the radio.

Remains. Even when they were talking about other things, I kept going back to the first thing they said. The worst thing. *They found remains at the cabin.*

In the rearview mirror, Ty's wide eyes meet mine. His skin is pale.

I try to think it through. "But I checked all the rooms of the cabin before I left. Nobody was there."

"You said it was trashed and you were in a hurry."

"I think I'd have noticed three bodies." The words come out with a sarcastic spin that makes him flinch. Earlier I imagined—and I pray I only imagined it, I pray it isn't some sort of memory—my family sprawled dead in the forest. What if the men had dragged them back into the cabin and then set the cabin on fire to cover up their crimes?

But thinking of dragging reminds me of something else. Someone else. And it's wrong that it makes me feel better to think of it. But what if the man in the oxblood shoes came back to figure out what had happened to Brenner, why he wasn't returning his calls? After he found him dead, he could have decided it was the perfect opportunity to cast more blame on me. He could have dragged Brenner back to the cabin before setting it on fire.

My mind whirls with possibilities. Am I an addict? A sweet girl? A girl who knows how to kill someone with her bare hands? What's a lie and what's the truth? I have no idea. But it sounds like the one woman who might be able to tell me is at the Winchester Hotel.

My aunt Elizabeth.

And we're only thirty minutes away from Portland.

CHAPTER 29
DAY 2, 5:08 P.M.

Once we're in Portland, we hit a Burger King drive-through (Ty refuses to even consider McDonald's), and then hunt for a pay phone. When we finally find one, he calls the Winchester Hotel and asks to be put through to Elizabeth Quinn. We decided it was safer to have a guy ask for her.

After he hangs up he walks back to where I'm sitting in the car. He's smiling.

"At first your aunt thought I was a reporter who missed the press conference. Then I explained who I was—and, more important, who I'm with. She's so happy to hear that you're okay. I tried to explain about how your memory's gone, but I don't think she totally understood. Still it sounds like she might know something about what's really going on."

Something inside me loosens. To finally know all the answers. To let an adult be in charge. I grin back at Ty.

Elizabeth said the safest thing would be to meet at the Winchester Hotel, so we park in the underground garage and then take the elevator up to the third floor. I take a deep breath and knock on the door of 312.

A slender woman dressed in cuffed skinny jeans, Doc Martens boots, and a long black sweater opens the door. She looks down the empty corridor and then pulls me inside. Ty's right on my heels. As soon as she closes the door, she hugs me.

"Oh, Cady!" Her arms are skinny and strong. "You've changed your hair!"

Encircled by her arms, I stiffen before our bodies make contact. I can't help it. I've finally found somebody who knows me, but I don't know her. Pulling back, she takes my cheeks in her hands and looks from one eye to the other, her face puzzled.

She has pale skin, shoulder-length black hair, and bright blue eyes set off by mascara and eyeliner. "Cady?" she says. "What's the matter?" She lets her hands fall away.

I don't say anything. I just stare at her face.

"It's like I told you on the phone," Ty says. "Cady doesn't remember anything that happened before late yesterday afternoon. We're pretty sure it's something called a fugue state. It happens when you've had a terrible shock. It takes your memories and locks them away so you can't access them, even though they're still there."

"And you don't remember anything? Anything at all?"

"I remember some stuff," I say. I feel oddly embarrassed, like I've been caught wearing nothing but a towel. "I remember the names of things, and how to walk and eat and drive. It's just that if it's something about me, then I can't remember it."

"So you don't even remember me?" She presses her lips together, looking hurt.

The longer I look at her, though, the more she *does* seem familiar. It's the shape of her cheekbones, the color of her eyes. "I'm pretty sure I remember your face," I say. "But nothing more than that. Sorry, Aunt Elizabeth."

She frowns. "Now I know you really don't remember me. You always called me Liz. So you don't remember your parents? Your brother?"

"I've got a picture of us, but I really don't remember them." My left temple is starting to throb.

She turns to Ty. "And, Ty, forgive me for asking, but how long have you known Cady?"

"I just met her last night. I could see she was in trouble, and I wanted to help her." He looks down at his shoes and then back up at Liz. In this room, with its formal, dark red wallpaper, he looks young and uncertain.

"Well, you've brought her to the right place." She rests her hand on my shoulder as if to show we're a team. "She's in good hands now."

I realize she's hinting that Ty should go. And maybe he should. But I don't want him to leave me with this woman I'm only starting to remember. Right now, Ty feels like my one friend in the world.

"Thanks, Liz." He says the words easily, but I can tell he's not going to budge. "I think I'll come along for the ride."

"I'm not sure that's such a good idea." She shakes her

head, setting her earrings in motion. "This is dangerous. Very dangerous. You don't want to get mixed up in it."

"I'm not going anywhere," Ty says. "Not until Cady is okay."

"What's dangerous?" I ask, massaging my temple. "What's going on? All I know is my family's missing and everyone but you seems to think I had something to do with it. But you said on the radio you were sure I didn't. How do you know?"

"Because your mom called me yesterday morning. She said she was on the run with your dad and Max, and asked me to help you. That's why I came to Portland. Holding the press conference was the only way I could think to reach out to you."

"So you talked to my mom?" I raise my head. Tears spark my eyes. "She's alive?"

"Janie and Patrick and Max are all okay." Liz bites her lip. "Or at least they were yesterday when Janie left me that message. She told me they were ditching their cell phones, so now I don't have any way to contact them. That's where I could use your help."

"My help? I can't even remember them."

"I think if we all put our pieces of the puzzle together, we can figure this thing out. Here, sit down and I'll try to explain." Liz sits on the edge of the bed, which is covered with a white duvet and tons of white pillows. Ty takes the chair that's in front of a small desk, turns it around, and straddles it. I sit in a maroon-striped wingback chair.

"First," Liz says, "tell me what you do know. Don't leave out anything, no matter how unimportant it seems."

So I tell her what we know and what we've been able to find out and what we've guessed. But there are a few parts I find myself glossing over. I don't tell her about the gun in my backpack or about how Michael Brenner died after I knocked him unconscious. If my aunt knew, would her opinion of me change? Would she still be so certain that I was in the right?

"Let me start by filling in the blanks," she says when I'm finished. "Maybe it will help you remember. Your parents work for a company called Z-Biotech. Does that sound familiar?"

It does! I straighten up, convinced that my memory is finally returning. And then—"I heard it on the news when we were driving here."

"And do you know what your parents do?"

"The radio said something about them being micro-biologists."

"Your parents are actually virologists. That means they work with viruses. To be honest, I don't completely understand exactly what they do. Hardly anyone does. But they're brilliant researchers." She sighs theatrically. "I took some science courses in college, but obviously my sister's the one who got the real brains in the family. Anyway, two years ago, in some remote part of Eastern Oregon, a girl who lived on a farm died. She was only nineteen. And then on the way to her funeral, her boyfriend got sick. Very sick. He ended up dying on the side of the road before the ambulance even showed up."

She takes a deep breath. "The autopsy report said he basically drowned in his own blood."

CHAPTER 30
DAY 2, 5:22 P.M.

My aunt watches my face intently. "Do you remember any of this so far?"

A disease that causes people to drown in their own blood? I shake my head. I don't. At least, I don't think I do. It's too hard to describe what I'm beginning to feel. Like trying to recall a dream a week after you have it. You've completely forgotten about it, and then the flash of a bird's wing or walking down a metal staircase conjures up part of your dream, bringing it into the real world. But only a few seconds feel sharp. The rest is still gone, and the more you try to remember, the less you succeed.

"Your parents were the ones who figured out it was a new strain of hantavirus that's being spread by field mice." She looks at me closely. "Does that sound familiar? Hantavirus?"

Slowly, I shake my head. Familiar isn't the word for what I'm feeling. It's more like dread.

"So the mice were biting people?" Ty asks.

"No," Liz says. "According to Janie, basically all a field mouse does is eat, poop, and have babies. And give hantavirus to each other when they mate or fight. Two years ago it rained a lot, which led to a huge wheat crop, which eventually led to an explosion in the field mice population. When it got hot, their droppings dried up. And then in barns and farms around Eastern Oregon, those powdery droppings got kicked up and inhaled. Eight people had the bad luck to breathe in those tiny particles, which carried hantavirus. Those people died."

"All of them?" Ty asks.

Liz sighs. "All of them. It's the most deadly strain of hantavirus ever discovered. It doesn't kill its hosts—the field mice—but it does kill humans." She turns to me. "It was your parents who figured it out. One person dying in one county, another in the next—it got misdiagnosed as pneumonia or the flu. But your parents had a hunch and began testing rodents in Eastern Oregon—the voles, the ground squirrels, the field mice—and figured out it was really a new strain of hantavirus."

"So?" Ty leans forward. "What does a disease carried by field mice have to do with men wanting to kill Cady?"

"Because her parents have also figured out the other half." Holding her hands facing each other, Liz links her fingers together, then looks at me over her interlaced fingers. "For the past year, your parents have been working on a vaccine for the new strain."

"But a vaccine's a good thing, isn't it?" I say. Then why do I feel so bad?

"Some vaccines do more than just keep you from catching a disease. Some also stop the virus in people who have already been exposed, but haven't gotten sick yet."

"That's how it works with rabies," Ty says. "And tetanus. If you give the shots to people soon enough after they've been bitten by a rabid animal or stepped on a rusty nail, they don't get sick."

"Right," Liz says, but her blue eyes never leave mine. "Last year, Z-Biotech was sold. The new owners weren't scientists, but Janie said they were fascinated with the idea that a vaccine could work even after exposure. They ordered your parents not to talk about the vaccine results, although it was working perfectly in animals. They said they didn't want to lose their market advantage." Her mouth twists. "Janie and Patrick are smart, but they live in their own little world. They didn't see that having both things—a devastating disease and the cure to that disease—could mean the makings of a weapon."

"A weapon?" Things are taking a turn I never imagined. "You mean like in war?" When Liz nods, I say, "But aren't those kinds of weapons illegal?" Her words are setting off echoes. Something about this conversation feels so familiar.

"Biological warfare was outlawed forty years ago," she says. "But it's not illegal to research how to defend against it."

Ty straightens up. "Aren't those things really two sides of the same coin?" he asks. "If you're researching how to defend yourself, couldn't that same research be used to figure out how to attack someone else?"

"Exactly. And the coin can get very thin at times." Liz beams at him and then turns to me. "This boy of yours is bright."

We both flush, for different reasons. He's not a boy and he's not mine.

"But what about the government?" I ask. "Don't they know what's going on?"

Liz shakes her head. "No one in the federal government keeps track of how many labs there are in the U.S., let alone what research they're doing. They do monitor a few pathogens, like anthrax. But hantavirus isn't one of them."

I think of Pandora's box. "But how could hantavirus be used as a weapon anyway? Wouldn't it just kill everyone once you started spreading it around? Hantavirus doesn't care who it kills."

"But it isn't spread from person to person," Liz says. "And with the vaccine, you could choose who didn't get sick after breathing in the virus."

I nod, but I'm not quite following.

Liz leans closer. "Okay, imagine a bomb, one that's filled with the droppings of infected field mice that have been dried out and pulverized. Which means trillions of infected particles have been weaponized. Say the bomb is set off in Country A's capital. In about four days, everyone who breathed in the particles—the president, the judges, the statesmen, and of course the citizens—starts to get sick. Muscle aches, fever, weakness. At first people think it's the flu. Only, ninety-five percent of them will die within a few days of exhibiting symptoms." She waits a minute for this to sink in.

"So during a war," I say, "a country could drop the bomb, kill everyone, and then send in vaccinated soldiers to clean up."

She nods. "There's another possibility, one that's less drastic. What if they set off the bomb and then offered people the vaccine in the first three days of exposure, before the symptoms start? That way no one would get sick, or if they did it would be mild."

"But what would be the point of that?" Ty asks.

"Before they got the vaccine, the government of Country A might have to meet certain demands. Maybe the government would have to step down. Or maybe they would have to give up their nuclear weapons."

"So our government wants this hantavirus and the vaccine?" Ty asks.

"A lot of people might want it," she says. "It could also be used on a smaller scale, say, putting the virus in the air vents of a shopping mall or a casino or a school. Or contaminating letters with powdered virus and sending them to the media or politicians or CEOs. Or renting a crop-duster and spraying the virus over a football stadium or a parade route. And if the people who inhale the virus want to live, they have to pay."

Ty puts his finger on something that had nagged me. "But if I didn't feel sick and you told me that in four days I was going to die from a disease I'd never heard of, why would I believe you?"

"Another good question," Liz says. "For it to work, a small number of people might need to be infected earlier. As an example of what could happen."

"As an example?" I echo. "But they would die! Who would do something that terrible? Terrorists?" I imagine men calling out to God as they press a lever.

"Or just people who want to make a lot of money." Liz looks from Ty to me. "How much would you pay for a cure if you knew you were going to die?"

CHAPTER 31
DAY 2, 5:52 P.M.

Ty and I don't say anything. We just look at each other. It's clear what the answer is. If you knew you were going to die, you would pay anything, do anything.

I feel dizzy. I don't know if it's from everything that's happened in the last two days, the headache, or what Liz just told us. Probably all three.

"Has Z-Biotech done anything with it yet?" Ty asks.

"Most of the first batch of vaccine went to animal testing and then, when that worked, on a few human volunteers at the lab. Now they're making a new vaccine, but it takes weeks. First you have to inject live virus into fertilized eggs and incubate them while the virus replicates. And then to make the vaccine, you have to mix embalming fluid with the liquid inside the eggs."

"That kills the virus," Ty says. "I've read about killed virus vaccines. Killed virus can't cause an infection but it will still kick the immune system into gear if someone is vaccinated with it."

Liz nods. "That's right. Janie was so excited when it looked like the vaccine might be successful. Then she and Patrick began to suspect what Z-Biotech was planning on doing with it. But they needed proof. If they made accusations that turned out to be wrong, their careers would be over. And without proof, Z-Biotech could just destroy the evidence. So they started secretly taking photos and going through files." My aunt's voice gets an edge. "I told Janie it wasn't safe. But you know your mother—she's stubborn. She said they were covering their tracks. But someone at Z-Biotech must have realized what they were doing."

"But what's happened to them since they called you?" It's hard for me to get the words out. "The radio said they found human remains in our family's cabin."

Liz leans forward and squeezes my hand. This time I don't pull away. "Oh, Cady, did you think it was them? That story was probably planted by Z-Biotech. Yesterday morning your parents went to work and got caught getting the last piece of evidence they needed. They took Max and left. They tried to warn you, but couldn't get in touch. So they left a bizarre message at your school to let you know something was wrong. And then they called and asked me to help you.

"But by the time I heard your mom's message, those two men had already grabbed you. Beaten you up. Searched your house. They wanted to know where the evidence or your parents were, but you said you didn't know." Her eyes search mine. "But now that you know what really happened, are you starting to remember?" She lets go of my hand.

150

"Maybe."

"Z-Biotech is not only looking for the evidence your parents took but for something else. Your parents are the only ones who have ever been successful in making a hantavirus vaccine. But they used some trick, some formula to make it work, and they told me they planned to take that with them. It's only in their heads, not on paper."

The pressure in my temple eases a little bit. "So now Z-Biotech won't be able to sell the virus and the vaccine to the highest bidder?"

"They still have a batch of vaccine in production, plus a little that was left over from the earlier testing. But that's it, unless Z-Biotech can find the formula. That must be why they searched the cabin, in case your parents had hidden anything there. But they found nothing, and you seemed to know nothing. So they decided to kill you. To them, you were as disposable as a piece of Kleenex."

Ty shakes his head and makes a wordless sound of protest.

"After you escaped, they knew they had to start spreading lies about you. That way, if you went to the police, they wouldn't believe a word you say." Her eyes never waver from my face. "But the thing is, Cady, I think you really do know something. I think your mind shut down to prevent you from telling those men. I think you know where your parents are or where they hid the information."

"I don't though." The throbbing in my temple is worse. "Or if I did, it's all gone. Some of what you said does sound familiar, but I can't remember any more than that."

"Please, Cady, you're the only chance we have to find my

sister. To find your family. Janie and Patrick must be holed up someplace, not sure whom they can trust. I know people who could help them. But that can't happen unless we find them or unless we can find evidence that proves what Z-Biotech is doing. And we can't let the company get to them or that information first."

"But I don't know anything." If only my head didn't hurt so much! My thoughts are muddled and slow. Everything my aunt says has set off echoes in me, but they're so faint and fleeting I can't grab hold of a single thought.

She stands up. I tilt my head to look at her. It feels like a stainless steel spike is being driven through my temple. "You know how I know you know something?"

"How?" I look past her at the fluffy white bed. If only I could climb under the covers and pull the pillows over my head. Block out the light, go to sleep, and forget the pain in my body and my mind.

"Because your parents prepared you. Look at how you knew how to disable this man, this Michael Brenner. The typical sixteen-year-old girl wouldn't know kung fu or karate or whatever you used."

"That just came out of nowhere," I say. It's still horrifying to think I killed a man. Killed him like I was on autopilot. "I didn't even know I knew how to do that until suddenly I was doing it."

"The same thing might happen with your mind. Maybe if you can get in the right space for it, you'll remember whatever it was they so desperately wanted to know." Liz nods, as if she has made a decision. "We should go to your house. Once you're in a familiar environment, things could come back to you."

"But seeing you didn't help," I point out. "It didn't change anything."

She frowns. "Yes, but it's not like we saw each other in person more than once every year or two. Being back in your house, the place where you lived with your family, the place where these men captured you—that could jog your memory. Maybe you'd even figure out where your parents might hide something."

Ty says, "But you said Z-Biotech already questioned Cady, and she didn't know anything then."

"But she was determined not to answer because she wanted to protect them. So determined she managed to lock everything away. I don't think Cady threw away the key. It's like Tyler said, Cady." She points at my head. "It's all still in there, someplace."

"Yeah, well, speaking of keys, I don't even have a key to my house." I think Liz is wrong. I think my memories are gone forever.

From the pocket of her jeans, she produces a silver house key. "I have one from when I house-sat for you while your family went on vacation in Hawaii." But after Ty gets to his feet, she says, "You should probably stay here, Ty. If anyone catches us, we could all end up in jail. Cady is a suspect in her parents' disappearance. At a minimum, you would be charged with aiding and abetting."

"I've come this far." Ty sets his jaw. I haven't even known him for a full day, but looking at his expression I know he won't be dissuaded. "I'm not leaving Cady, not now."

"But you're the one who stole the car in Bend," Liz points out. "That's a felony."

He walks over to me and puts his hand under my elbow. "That doesn't matter. I'm not leaving Cady."

CHAPTER 32
DAY 2, 6:21 P.M.

Liz's car, a sleek dark blue Avalon, is parked not far from where we left the Subaru. I sit in front with my hood pulled up. Ty sits behind me.

At first, I try to recognize landmarks, the signs and buildings and businesses in the center of the city, even though I hadn't when we first drove into town. I rest my forehead against the cool glass and ignore my pounding head. Everyone is quiet, and the radio isn't on, so I don't have to worry about hearing my name. The sole sound in the car is the *swish-swish* of the wipers.

It's only after I give up, after Liz turns the car in to a neighborhood of older two-story houses with porches and yards and the occasional basketball hoop that something begins to stir in the back of my mind.

Am I imagining it, or do things look familiar? Or maybe every city has a neighborhood that looks like this.

My index finger is pressed into my temple, providing a counterpoint to the pain inside.

Lost in my own thoughts, I'm startled when Liz pulls over and parks. "Your house is just up the block," she says. "We'll go in the back. Quickly, in case one of the neighbors thinks you really are some sociopathic killer." She surveys the empty street before she gets out of the car. The rain is now coming down hard enough to discourage anyone from being outside.

We run through the downpour toward a two-story green house with solar panels on the roof. The house sits silent and dark. Yellow crime scene tape crosses the front door. Three brick steps lead to the porch. On the top one, a pumpkin sits to one side, grinning.

Wait. That pumpkin. I know there's a fat white candle inside of it, surrounded by a puddle of blackened wax. Or *do* I know that? Am I just imagining it? And if there really is a candle, what does that prove? It would be easy enough to guess. We dart around the side of the house, past a white-curtained window, then two panes set higher, as if over a sink, each with a window box full of herbs. The herbs are being bruised by the rain, and their green scent hangs in the air.

Liz puts her key into the lock of the back door, also crisscrossed by crime scene tape. Ty touches my arm, and I jump. Does anything seem familiar? I feel like I'm seeing double, what's here now layered over a fainter image of what used to be. Liz pushes the door open, and we duck under the crime scene tape. We're in the kitchen, but it's been trashed.

A piece of pink paper pinned on the refrigerator catches my eye. I know I've seen it before. That it was important to me. I walk over to it, my feet crunching over cereal, flour, coffee grounds, and shards of broken glass.

"Cady?" Ty says. I don't turn around.

It's a poster. In the middle is a photo of a stack of mattresses. Standing next to the stack is a guy dressed like a king, wearing a silver crown and a long robe with black-spotted white fur cuffs and collar. On top of the mattresses sits a girl, cross-legged. She's leaning over to rest her chin on the top of the king's head. She's got a crown, too, but it looks cartoonish, and her hair is divided into two very non-royal pigtails. Across the top it says, "Wilson High Presents: *Once Upon a Mattress.*"

The girl is me.

I'm an actress.

Don't act. Be.

And now I can put a face with those words that have been echoing in my head for the past two days. In my memory, I see a middle-aged man with a clipboard sitting in an otherwise empty auditorium, looking up at me on a stage. I can't remember anything else he said, or whether I was alone or not. But I remember how his words resonated.

My head hurts so much I have to close my left eye. I turn in a circle, looking at the rest of the house without seeing it, not the drawers emptied and thrown on the floor, not the ripped-up carpet, the scattered papers, the sliced uphol-stery.

"What is it, Cady?" Liz asks eagerly. "Are you remembering something?"

"I'm not sure."

She steps closer and grips my wrist. "What do you think those men wanted? What did they think you knew?"

I feel like I'm going to fly apart. "I don't know."

"Do you think your parents could have hidden the information here in the house? If we can find it, we would have a bargaining chip to get Z-Biotech to leave them alone. There must be something you know. A hiding place where they might keep a safe-deposit box key or a flash drive. I know your parents told you something, Cady, but until you tell me what it was we can't help them."

Without answering Liz, I shake my head and pull my wrist away. It's all up to me, and I'm failing. My stupid brain won't cough up part of an answer. Won't even hint. Where would my parents go? Where would they hide something?

"Well, where do you think they are?" Liz's face is only inches from mine. "Did they leave you a phone number? A code word? Is there a friend they might have gone to? We can't help them if we can't find them."

I press my fingers against my temple so hard I'm sure I'm leaving bruises. In my mind's eye, I see more flickers of memories. A little boy blowing out birthday candles. The man who is my father pointing at something, his face serious. The woman from the photo in my backpack standing over this very stove, holding out a wooden spoon for me to taste.

"I don't know," I say. "I don't know, I don't know, I don't know."

"Come on, Cady," she urges. "Surely you remember something."

I'm so overwhelmed by the mingling of past and present that it takes me a long moment to answer her. "No." I need to explain that it's all still like a dream or a nightmare, bits and pieces that don't make any sense. I'm opening my mouth when her face tightens.

"All right," she says firmly, and she steps back and pulls a gun from her purse. Ty lets out a gasp. "If you're going to be like that." Not taking her eyes off us, she calls out, "Michael?"

And Michael Brenner, the man I killed, steps in from the hall.

I cry out and put my hands over my eyes as my memories come flooding back.

CHAPTER 33

EIGHT WEEKS AGO

I was supposed to be doing homework when my dad knocked on the door of my room. "Okay if I come in?"

I clicked off the YouTube video I had been watching on my laptop and back onto the screen with my English essay. "Sure."

But when he pushed open the door, my mom was standing in the hall behind him. What was up? They seldom came into my room together, unless I was in really big trouble. Last May, when I had skipped school and taken off to the coast for the day with some friends, they had talked to me at the same time. Or talked *at* me. But what had I done lately that would cause them to look so serious?

My dad took a deep breath. "Your mother and I have been around and around about this." They exchanged a glance I couldn't read. "But we have to tell you at some point, and you're old enough to know."

A door closed in my head. Closed tight. Part of me had been wondering and worrying that this day was coming. Lately, it had been so obvious that something was wrong at our house. The closed doors, the muffled arguments, the conversations that turned into whispers or were dropped altogether when I came into a room. So which one would I end up living with? Would I have to move?

They still weren't saying anything. Why couldn't my parents just do it quick and clean, like pulling off a Band-Aid?

I decided to do it for them. "You're getting a divorce."

My dad blinked.

"What? No." My mom shook her head. "It's nothing like that." She laughed a little, but it sounded sad. Her eyes were unfocused. "If only it were that."

"Then what is it?" But my mind supplied another answer, even worse. "One of you has cancer?" My veneer of not caring shattered.

My dad threw up his hands. "Will you just let us talk?" The words exploded out of his mouth.

I shrank back in my chair. My dad never yelled. Never. Not even when I had been grounded for a month after the whole skipping school to go to the coast thing.

My mom laid a hand on his arm. "Patrick, you're scaring her."

He turned to her, speaking as if I wasn't there. "I have to scare her, don't I? She has to realize how serious this is. If we put one foot wrong, it could be the end for all of us." He turned back to me. "Do you know what we do at work?"

"Research. In a lab. Into animal diseases." I had no idea where this was going. Just that I was starting to shake.

Whatever they were going to tell me was worse than divorce. Worse than cancer. "Viruses." I had visited them once, four years ago, for Take Your Daughter to Work day. I had had to put on vinyl gloves, a paper suit, and a breathing mask, and I had to promise a million times that I wouldn't touch anything without permission. I had gotten to feed the hamsters and the rats and even the monkeys they kept in the basement. Then a year ago, the company had been bought by another, bigger company. I hadn't paid that much attention. All I knew was that my parents didn't like their new bosses.

"Right." He nodded. "And in the course of our research, your mother and I made a discovery." My dad took my mom's hand and squeezed it, then turned back to me. "We don't want to tell you too much. It could be dangerous for you if we did. If things go bad, not knowing anything might be the only thing that saves you. At first it was just a promising development. But then we realized that the new owners of Z-Biotech are thinking of exploiting it." His voice shook. "It's actually worse than that. If what we're thinking they're doing is true, then—"

"Patrick." My mom touched his arm again. "We said we weren't going to tell Cady too much."

I was frustrated by their unfinished sentences, by their hints. "What? You have to tell me something."

My mom took a deep breath. "We need to stop the company before it's too late. What they're doing is not just illegal, but it could have devastating consequences for . . ." Her voice trailed off. "For everything. For thousands of people. Maybe millions. Do you understand?"

I didn't understand anything. Only that I wished this was a dream. Even a nightmare because at least then I could wake up. I shook my head.

"Diseases can be used as weapons," my dad said. "Remember when we talked about that when you took European history last year?"

He had tried to get me to see that history was more than a list of dates and battles, dry facts, the boring language of treaties. So he had told me that in the Middle Ages, besiegers had catapulted the corpses of the plague dead over castle walls. During the French and Indian War, Native Americans had deliberately been given blankets from a smallpox hospital. With no natural immunity, about 90 percent of the ones who caught smallpox died.

I nodded.

"Z-Biotech wants to use something we discovered in bad ways," he said. "And we need to find a way to stop them."

My mind whirled, not able to come to rest on anything. I wished it were still five minutes ago, and I was watching three high school guys dressed in coconut-shell bras and grass skirts badly lip-syncing to a popular song.

"So go to the police." But even I knew that probably wasn't the answer. The police probably wouldn't understand. My parents had done post-doctorate work in clinical microbiology and virology. Only a few people in the world really understood what they did. And most of those people worked at Z-Biotech. "Or, I don't know, go to the government. Aren't there programs for whistle-blowers?"

"We don't know who we can trust." My dad scraped his

hands back through his hair, so that it stuck up in tufts. "Some people in the government might actually support what Z-Biotech is doing, especially if it could be used against America's enemies. And we need proof. They'll destroy or hide the evidence long before anyone shows up to inspect things."

My mother's face was like a stone. "And if Z-Biotech ever figures out that we're collecting information, we could be killed. All of us. Not just your father and me, but you and Max."

An icy finger traced my spine. "But Max is just a little kid. What kind of people would murder a child?"

My mom's jaw tightened. "The reason we're talking to you is because of what happened to the Radleys."

My eyes went wide. Mrs. Radley—Barbara—had worked at Z-Biotech, too, had been good friends with my mom. Miranda Radley had only been a year younger than me, a pudgy, quiet girl who liked to read books about were-wolves and fallen angels. Her brother, Alex, was two years older than me. He had black bangs that fell across his green eyes, somehow managing to draw attention to them instead of hiding them.

A month earlier, the Radleys—the parents and Miranda and Alex and even their Labradoodle—had all died in a house fire when a pile of rags used to refinish some furniture had caught fire on their deck. An unusually warm night, paint fumes, spontaneous combustion. . . . It had been a terrible tragedy.

Hadn't it?

We had all attended their funeral, even Max. My mom's

164

eyes had been swollen from weeping. She kept wiping her cheek on Max's hair until he squirmed away. Then she pressed her fist to her mouth like a stopper. My dad had been stoic, a muscle flickering in his jaw.

"Barbara had her doubts," Mom said now. "She made the mistake of taking them higher up the food chain. The fire did three things: It made sure she never told; it destroyed any evidence she might have collected; and it sent a message to anyone at Z-Biotech who was getting a little too curious."

My bones turned to water. "Then quit. Just quit your jobs. You can find something else to do."

My dad gave a short, bitter laugh. "It's not that easy. Six months ago, Derek Chambers died in a diving accident in Hawaii, just ran out of air. Everyone said it was a freak accident. But he had been talking about leaving the company."

I was shaking, shaking like I had walked into a deep freeze. "Then don't say anything. Don't do anything."

"We can't, Cady." My mom's voice was soft and patient. "We thought about that, but we just can't. We have to do what's right. Not just for us, but for you, too. What they're thinking of doing could kill thousands of innocent people. As soon as we have enough information to prove it, we'll take steps to stop them. But until then, everything has to be normal. You can't tell anyone."

"Then why are you telling me now?" Anger swelled in me, and in a strange way I welcomed it. "I can't do anything about it, I can't tell anybody, and I might even be killed. Frankly, I'd have preferred not to know."

"We're telling you so that you'll have a chance to save yourself if something goes wrong," my dad said. "If anyone ever tells you to go with them, don't, no matter what they say. Do whatever you have to and get away from them. Go to the police. If we're missing, they'll listen to you. And just being with the cops might be enough to discourage these people from coming after you."

My mom added, "And if you ever come home and it looks like someone has been going through our stuff, just turn around and leave immediately."

My voice was small. "I'm scared."

"It won't be for long," my dad said. "Maybe only a couple of months. We're moving very carefully, covering our tracks. And once we have the evidence and have figured out where to go with it, then we'll take action."

"Until then, I've signed the three of us up for individual instruction at the Multnomah Academy of Martial Arts." My mom's face was determined. "We're getting an alarm system installed, and your dad is going to buy a gun."

A gun! Now I knew something was really wrong. My parents didn't like guns.

"If we ever get separated, we'll figure out a way to reconnect." Mom moved closer and stroked my hair. "But don't worry. We won't let that happen."

That memory is awful. But the one that follows is even worse. Because now I know why I forgot.

The reason my brain shut down?

It's because the person I love most in the world is dead.

CHAPTER 34

DAY 1, 8:12 A.M.

Yesterday morning, I had just gotten off the city bus outside of Wilson High when I reached in my jacket pocket for my phone and found only my house key. Crap! My phone was still on the charger on my desk. I hesitated. Should I go back for it and miss first period? Or stay and not have a phone all day?

My first class was Honors French. Madame Aimée seldom took roll, so even if I didn't show up, there was a good chance it wouldn't be reported. And these days, my mom was so anxious. She wanted to know where I was at all times. She'd freak out if she looked at the tracker on my phone and saw I was still at home but wasn't answering my phone. I crossed the street and waited for the next bus that would take me back.

By the time I put my key in the lock a half hour later, my mind was somewhere else. Although my parents had warned me, I wasn't looking for signs that things were terribly wrong. Mentally, I was already back at school, wondering if it would be worthwhile to go to French for just ten minutes.

I took two steps inside the door. Just as I registered that the alarm wasn't going off, waiting for me to go to the panel to silence it, something wet and sweet pressed against my face. I took in half a breath and then my world went dark.

When I woke up, everything was still dark. Only, it was dark green. My head was covered by cloth that was tight around my shoulders.

I realized that I was tied to one of our dining room chairs. I was afraid to move. It seemed important that whoever had done this to me not know I was awake. Behind me, I heard the noise of people searching and destroying—crashing, cracking, ripping, splintering, slicing. And judging by the swearing, not finding anything. Men's voices. Two, I thought, or maybe three.

My mind raced, trying to figure a way out of this. My parents had been paying for private self-defense lessons with an ex-Marine. Kevin had taught me how to defend myself against almost anything, up to and including a man with a gun. But even his instruction hadn't covered waking up with your hands tied behind your back, your ankles lashed to a chair, and a pillowcase pulled over your head.

A cloth had been stuffed into my open mouth and now rested against my tongue. But I must have made some soft, small sound because footsteps came up behind me. Suddenly someone slapped my ears with open palms. For a moment, my head was transformed into the inside of a bass drum, hollow and percussive.

The gag muffled my scream.

A man's whisper slid into my ear. "Where are your parents, Cady?"

I shook my head, the fabric of the pillowcase rubbing my cheeks. I truly didn't know the answer, but I wouldn't have given it to him if I did. I remembered the Radleys—Alex and Miranda and their parents.

"Don't scream," he warned, "or I'll shoot you." For a moment, he rested something cold and hard between my eyes. The tip of a gun. Then his hand snaked under the pillowcase and slowly tugged the gag from my mouth, like a magician producing a scarf. Enough light came from the bottom of the pillowcase that I could see it was the yellow dishcloth that this morning had been hanging on our refrigerator door. My mouth was dry, my tongue a piece of leather.

"Where are your parents?" he repeated. His tone was reasonable.

"I don't know. At work?" I tried to gauge how close he was. If I head-butted him the right way, it was possible that I could knock him out and stay conscious myself. But what good would that do me? I could still hear the sounds of people searching behind me.

He grabbed my ear through the pillowcase and twisted, squeezing it like a lemon. "Don't play stupid, Cadence. It doesn't suit you."

"I honestly don't know where they are." It was the truth, but it felt like a lie.

For an answer, he grabbed my arm, just above the elbow. His fingers dug in. I could feel my muscles separate. And then he found a nerve bundle. An electric shock jolted up my arm. I let out a yelp.

I didn't know this man. I memorized his smooth voice, his faintly perfumed smell, his expensive shoes. I could see them in a gap at the bottom of the pillowcase. I studied them for clues. They were a graduated reddish brown color I thought was called oxblood. They looked like the shoes a successful businessman would wear, not a killer. But I had no doubts that was what he was.

"Where is the information about the virus and the vaccine?" he said.

"I don't know what you're talking about." If my parents had told me more, would I have been spilling it? I hoped not.

He hit me then. Punched me in the jaw. I felt one of my teeth move. My mouth tasted like metal.

"Stop lying to me! I've already had to do bad things today, Cady. Very bad things. I don't want to have to do any more."

Bad things? What did he mean?

But he didn't give me time to think about it. His tone changed. It was like he was playing both roles: good cop and bad cop. Only there was no one on the other side of a one-way mirror to stop him from going too far.

"Where would they hide something? A girl like you, a smart girl, you must know where your parents hide things."

"I don't know." I tried not to let the strain sound in my voice. "I don't know anything. If they hid something, I don't know where it is."

"Do they have a safe-deposit box?"

"I have no idea."

Again, he took my left ear in his hand and squeezed it. Then he whispered into it. "Cady." A pause filled by nothing but his breath. "Pretending you don't know anything won't help you."

"But I don't know anything."

He sighed as he straightened up. Then he slapped the back of my head. I tried not to make any noise, but a grunt pushed through my teeth.

I felt him lean closer again. "I'm going to put the gun up against your head again and next time you lie to me I'll pull the trigger."

I was telling the truth, but he thought it was a lie. Should I try to really lie? Should I make up a place my parents might have gone, or a place they would hide things, just to buy myself time? But if I did, it would backfire sooner or later. Probably sooner. And if I sent them running off on a wild-goose chase, how many others might end up tied to a chair with a gun pressed against their heads?

"Have they told anyone else?"

I decided not to pretend I didn't know what he was talking about. "I don't know. I honestly don't know!"

"Stop lying," he said, and cursed me. His slap jerked my head to one side. "Stop lying or the same thing will happen to you that already happened to your little brother."

I froze. "What are you talking about?"

His voice was flat. "He's dead."

What? My little brother, dead? It couldn't be true. Not

Max. Not Max with his smile so big that his brown eyes nearly disappeared.

"What use was a crying child to us? He couldn't help us. And I'm starting to think you are just as useless. The same thing will happen to you if you don't tell me something useful. Now!"

"Max can't be dead," I said. Pushing away the thought of how this man had just boxed my ears and slapped and slugged me. Pushing away the memory of the gun pressing between my eyes.

"You want proof?" the man with the oxblood shoes said roughly. "I'll give you proof."

He walked out of the room. Behind me, he spoke to someone. It sounded like they were arguing. Their words were too low for me to make out, but I memorized the timbre of their voices.

"They're bringing his body," he told me. "So you'll know I'm telling the truth."

I was too stunned to speak. The pillowcase in front of my face was now wet, slimy with tears and snot. How could this be happening to me? Already French class seemed like something that happened in another world, another universe.

A minute or an hour later, I heard voices. A knife sawed at the tie that held my hands. I could hear it cutting into the wood of the chair. I didn't care that one more thing in our house was being ruined. I didn't care that in a few minutes my hands would be free, although my legs were still tied up and at least one man had a gun. I didn't care that there must be some combination of moves that would leave me able to run and my attackers too disabled to pursue me.

Max couldn't be dead. Could he?

Something heavy and yet somehow soft landed on the table.

"Touch him," the man with the oxblood shoes ordered. "Touch your brother."

I kept my hands where they were. My whole body was shaking.

He grabbed my hand and began to force it up. "Max is dead. And you're next if you don't tell me what I need to know."

I tried to pull away, but he was stronger than me. Through a sheet of plastic my fingers touched something. A leg or an arm. Firm, but yielding. And cool. Then he moved my fingers so that they touched my brother's hand. His poor little hand, fingers curled and stiff.

Max was dead. They had killed my brother.

Max. He weighed thirty-three pounds. You wouldn't think you could pack so much life into just thirty-three pounds. His giggle, his imagination, his sudden hungers for ice cream or piggyback rides or stories. He bounced rather than walked. He was always waving an imaginary wand and proclaiming he had just turned me into a frog or a butterfly or a witch.

Max was dead.

My brother was dead.

And with my fingertips still touching his cold, dead hand, my mind shut down. Went blank. Went someplace where I wouldn't have to remember. Even when they pulled out my fingernails, it wouldn't come back.

CHAPTER 35
DAY 2, 6:48 P.M.

The scream that tears itself from my throat sounds like an animal's.

Now I remember everything, but I would rather be dead myself than know that my little brother, Max, is.

"You killed him!" I scream at Brenner. "You killed Max." The pieces are falling into place. Brenner and the man with the oxblood shoes were the men who searched my house, the men who took me to the cabin to search there and then tortured me again when they found nothing and I told them nothing. They're the ones who killed my little brother and stuffed his body in a plastic bag like a piece of garbage.

With a wordless cry, I launch myself at him.

He takes a half step back, his eyes uncertain. Flesh-colored makeup doesn't hide the red scratches running the length of his face or the wine-colored bruises under his eyes.

I don't care that Elizabeth has a gun pointed at me. All I care about is getting my hands on one of the men who killed my brother.

Before he can decide what to do, I grab his wrist and step behind him. In one motion, I pull his arm out and up, rolling the knife edge of my free hand along the nerve bundle just under his biceps. He falls to his knees at the same time as I brace his arm across my thighs.

Red rage clouds my vision, hums in my ears. He killed Max! I don't think, I just act. With the heel of my hand, I break his arm, right at the elbow.

His scream is high-pitched and wordless. I stare down at the back of his head, which has been shaved and covered with a white bandage, and feel . . . nothing.

Nothing at all.

"Let Michael go!" Elizabeth has to yell to be heard over his keening. "Or I'll shoot your friend." I look up. She's grabbed Ty's shoulder and her gun is now pointed at his head.

As ordered, I stand up and back away. Brenner screams again when his limp hand hits the floor. Then he pulls it to his chest and cradles it, rocking back and forth. "I'm not a killer," he moans. "I'm a computer scientist."

I'm filled with an icy clarity as I look from the man who killed my brother to the woman who brought me here. While her face is still familiar, I know for sure that she's not my aunt. My mother has only one sibling, her brother. My uncle Joe. He lives in St. Louis.

"And who are you?"

"My name is Elizabeth Tanzir," she says, raising her chin.

"I'm Z-Biotech's senior vice president of marketing. Quinn was your mother's maiden name." Now I remember where I've seen her before. My mom had let me borrow her car if I took her to work, and I had seen Mom talking with this woman outside the building. "We need to find your parents before they ruin everything. We offered to trade your life for the information they stole, but clearly they thought the information was more important, since they never even bothered to come to the cabin. At that point you were worthless to us."

I don't mean to, but I make a small noise. Something that betrays how much her words hurt. My brother is dead and my parents abandoned me to the mercy of his killers.

"But the fact that you are some kind of martial arts expert made us realize you might actually know more than you've told us. Maybe even more than you thought you knew."

As she speaks, out of the corner of my eye, I see Ty slowly beginning to shift his stance. As soon as I notice it, I fasten my gaze on Elizabeth's face so as not to give him away.

"After all, if you were just some innocent, how were you able to disable a grown man? Our chief of information technology." Her lips pull back in disgust as she regards Brenner, who is still on his knees, cradling his broken arm. "Since force hadn't worked with you, I suggested we try a different approach. If something inside of you had shut down rather than betray your parents, maybe it would open up again if you thought you were really helping them." She makes a huffing sound. "But it's clear you really *don't* know anything."

Just as the words leave her mouth, Ty grabs for her gun. Trying to keep it from him, Elizabeth swings her arm wildly. In the space of a few seconds, it points at Ty, at me, even at Brenner. Ty manages to force her hand up, up, up, and the gun goes off, sounding like a thunderclap. Bits of plaster rain down. But she still won't let go of it.

There's no time to take off my backpack and find my gun. My eyes sweep around the room, looking for something I can smash over her head. On the dining room table, something glints. In two strides I'm standing where the man with the oxblood shoes cut my bonds so he could force me to touch my brother's dead hand. I snatch up the paring knife he used and run up behind Elizabeth, who is still tussling with Ty. At the touch of the blade on her neck, she freezes.

"Let Ty have the gun," I say.

There's a long moment where I can feel her weighing what to do.

"Better do it, Aunty Liz." I press the knife a fraction of an inch. Her skin dimples, resists, and then finally begins to part just the tiniest bit. But it's not until a trickle of blood snakes down her neck that she lets go.

Ty trains the gun on her.

She steps back, her arms crossed. "So if you know I'm not your aunt, you must remember everything now," she says.

"The thing is," I tell her, "there's nothing to remember. My parents didn't tell me anything. They were trying to protect me. So the only things I remember are how you tortured me. And how you killed my brother. How could you

177

kill a three-year-old child?" I resist the urge to push the paring knife to see just how far it will go into her neck. Instead, my voice breaks. "What did Max ever do to you? Couldn't you have just tied him up or something?"

"What are you talking about?" Ty's hand tightens on the grip of the gun. "They killed your little brother?"

"Everything happened just the way Elizabeth said. Except she left out one little detail. When I was tied up and blindfolded, they brought me my brother's body and made me touch it. They told me they would kill me just like they had my brother if I didn't tell them where my parents were or where they had hidden the information. They thought it would get me to talk. Instead, it just made me go into that fugue state."

Elizabeth's laugh sounds like a rusty hinge. "The human mind is very suggestible. Did you ever play that game at Halloween? The one where you put your hand in a bowl of peeled grapes, but you're told they're eyes?"

"What?" The headache is back, full force. Why is she talking about holidays and games?

"We don't have your brother. We never did. I have no idea if he's dead or alive, but if he's dead, we didn't do it."

"I felt his body!"

"You had a pillowcase over your head. What you felt was a chimp."

I can't take in what she's saying. "What?"

"When it became clear you wouldn't cooperate, Kirk had me bring one of our dead animal specimens here. He was sure it would break you. All it did was push you over the edge. Even when they yanked your fingernails out at the cabin, you wouldn't say anything. And after your parents didn't take Kirk up on a trade, well, at that point you were nothing but a nuisance."

To who? I wonder numbly. To my parents as well as the people from Z-Biotech? I can't pull myself together enough to ask questions. I feel dizzy. Max was dead, and now he is alive again. Or is he? Elizabeth says my parents abandoned me to the thugs from Z-Biotech. Or maybe the reason my parents didn't come for me is because they couldn't. Has something bad happened to them, something the Z-Biotech people don't know about yet?

"Who's Kirk?" Ty asks.

"Kirk Nowell. Our CEO."

"She was tortured by the CEO for Z-Biotech?" Ty sounds incredulous.

Elizabeth shrugs. "The company was going down the tubes when we bought it. It took someone with vision to see what could be done with the raw materials. Kirk was that person. Sometimes the ends do justify the means. And in this case, our end goal is to make a lot of money."

"How were you planning on spending it?" Ty asks. "Money's not all that useful in jail."

Her smile is condescending. "Do you know how many countries don't have an extradition treaty with the United States? There are half a dozen with a low cost of living and beautiful beaches. Places where a little American money would go a long way, and where, if you bribe the right people, they are willing to look the other way."

"So where is Kirk?" I ask. "Does he know you're here?"

"My job was to find out what you knew and then take care of you. Make it look like you killed the boy you had tricked into helping you and afterward killed yourself." Despite a gun and a knife pointed in her direction, Elizabeth smiles. "And Kirk will be expecting us to report back soon."

CHAPTER 36

DAY 2, 7:02 P.M.

I wish I could take back breaking Brenner's arm. While it's made him as compliant as a five-foot-nine toddler, he's also nearly as weepy and whiny as one. Ty says because of all the nerves and veins that run through the joint, a broken elbow is known to be one of the most painful injuries. By the way Brenner's behaving, I can believe it. He mostly rocks back and forth, moaning "It hurts, it hurts, it hurts," while Ty and I take turns dealing with Elizabeth. I search her— thoroughly—but she doesn't have any more weapons. In her purse, I find her keys, cell phone (from which I remove the battery), and a Z-Biotech ID card on a lanyard.

After a whispered conference with Ty, we decide to tie up the two of them in my parents' room while we figure out what to do next. We can't leave them in the living room or they'll be in view of anyone who comes to the front door. Brenner manages to stagger to his feet and then shuffles down the hall. Elizabeth is quieter—quiet enough that I watch her closely.

"Take my gun while I tie her up," Ty says, handing it over. I tuck it in my waistband and never take my eyes off Elizabeth—or my finger off the trigger of the gun I retrieved from my backpack.

"Why did they say there were human remains in my family's cabin?" I ask Elizabeth as Ty ties her wrists tight with one of my mom's scarves.

She doesn't answer, so I kick a nerve bundle on her outer thigh. She sees the look on my face and decides it's not worth not talking.

"Kirk threw the chimp in the trunk when he and Michael took you out to the cabin to look for your family. He figured it would raise too many questions if it were found at your house. After you assaulted Michael, they decided to burn down the cabin . . . with the chimp's body inside. They figured it would make the authorities more eager to find you."

"And who shot Officer Dillow?"

"That security guy?" She shrugs. "Kirk. Kirk said that guy asked way too many questions—especially for a rent-a-cop."

I squeeze my eyes closed, but only for a second. Someday I'll have time to think about Officer Dillow, who died because he tried to help me.

"Do you have anything else you want to ask her?" Ty says. I can tell he's tired of listening to her. When I shake my head, he gags her with one of my dad's ties. "This will keep her from planning anything with Brenner."

"Good idea."

Even though Brenner, who's leaning against the wall with his arm cradled against his chest, doesn't look like he would be capable of planning a walk down the hall, I don't want Elizabeth to know how much she gets to me. She said my parents didn't come to the cabin because they didn't care. That can't be true, can it? But what if the real reason they didn't come is even worse?

With more ties, Ty lashes Elizabeth's hands to the bedpost. He doesn't leave her any slack and she doesn't look very comfortable.

Which bothers me not one little bit.

Next, we deal with Brenner, who is panting and pale. When he opens his eyes and sees us regarding him, both of us holding guns, he mumbles again, "I didn't want to do any of this. I'm a computer scientist, not a killer."

I'm not feeling too sympathetic.

"We can't just leave his arm like that," Ty says, as we look at him. "If we don't splint it, he could end up with nerve damage. Plus I think he's going into shock."

"Aren't you forgetting something?" I whisper. "He wanted to kill me."

"We're better than the bad guys are, remember?"

I stop arguing with Ty and go look for the supplies he needs. From our camping stuff, I get a sleeping pad he can use to splint the arm. From the linen closet, dishtowels to tie the splint in place. And from the floor in front of the dresser, my dad's socks, to cushion Brenner's arm. I wonder what my parents will say when they find out their things were used to give aid and comfort to the enemy.

I just hope they're still alive to learn it.

Brenner lets out a muffled scream when Ty splints his arm. My would-be killer is sweaty and pale. With his scratches, bruises, and bandages, he looks like the real victim.

Eyes dull with pain, Brenner says, "They told me we would be rich. And that no one would die."

"Uh-huh." I let my sarcasm show. He obviously abandoned that idea by the time he started dragging me out to the woods.

Ty has Brenner lie on the floor with his feet on the bed, on the opposite side from Elizabeth. He ties one ankle and the unbroken arm to the bed frame, making sure that there isn't any way for Elizabeth to reach Brenner or vice versa.

Watching Ty work gives me time to think. Even though it seems that I have all the missing pieces of my memory— before and after the fugue state—I still feel like there's something I'm missing. Some clue that I'm completely overlooking.

I run through it again in my head. My parents are on the run from Z-Biotech with my little brother. They have proof that Z-Biotech—in particular, the two people in this room, plus Kirk Nowell—had plans to exploit the virus and the vaccine. Had plans to sell it to someone to potentially kill thousands of people.

Ty finishes and comes over to me. Brenner's eyes are closed, his breathing shallow and fast. Elizabeth is watching us. I want to get away from those bright blue eyes. "Do you think it's safe to leave them alone?"

Ty shrugs slightly. "For a while anyway."

"Let's go to my room and figure out what to do next. I don't like her watching us."

My bed's not made, but at least this room isn't as trashed as the rest of the house. I kick some discarded clothes under the bed as I pull up the orchid-colored silk comforter. Ty does a good job of pretending not to notice. Instead he looks at the walls, which feature posters for plays I've been in, as well as black and yellow covers of Playbills from the two times I've been to New York.

"So you're an actress?" he says.

"I think it kind of came in handy the last few days." I sigh as I sit down at my desk. My phone is still plugged into the charger. The last time I was here, I was doing chemistry homework. The thought seems surreal. I rub my temple. "I feel like I'm missing something. I think one of the things somebody told me when I couldn't remember wasn't right. Only I didn't know enough to know that it wasn't."

"That's going to be hard to sort out," Ty says as he sits down on the edge of my bed. "Everyone's been lying to you or about you."

I run through the last two days in my mind. And then I finally realize what it is.

"Remember when we were at the library and read that article about me?"

"Well, that whole thing was wrong, wasn't it? I mean, you didn't shoot Dillow and you didn't hurt your family," Ty says.

"That's not what I'm thinking about. It's that message it said my parents left at the school. They said I sold their car."

"They just said that to warn you to stay away from the house."

"But why make up a story about me selling a Datsun? Now that I've got my memory back, I know we don't own a Datsun. My dad's first car was a Datsun, and he used to talk about it, but they haven't made that brand for years and years. So why would my parents make up such a weirdly specific detail? Did the reporter get it wrong?" I straighten up. "Or was it a code?" As I talk, I go to Craigslist for Portland. I click on the "cars and trucks" section. There are thousands of listings. But when I type "Datsun" in the search box, there are only twenty-two listed.

I scan down. The third entry from the bottom is for a '97 Datsun. It sticks out because it's a decade newer than any of the other listings. I click. And there it is. The last desperate message from my parents.

In its entirety, the listing reads, "'97 Datsun with 15,550 miles. Only 2 owners. Please call between 2 and 7 pm."

"How can a car that old have so few miles?" Ty asks.

I don't answer because I'm busy writing down each of the numbers mentioned in the ad: 97 15,550 2 2 7.

He looks closer. "And how is anyone supposed to call if there's no phone number?"

"Because the whole ad is basically a phone number!" I tell him as I snatch up my cell phone and start pushing the numbers 971-555-0227. "My parents were trying to tell me how to contact them." My heart is beating fast as I push the final seven. The phone rings only once, and then it switches to a recorded message. It's a man's voice repeating the phone number I just dialed, followed by a beep.

But I recognize that voice.

I start to say something, but the words get caught in my throat.

"Dad? Daddy? It's me, Cady. I'm okay. I hope you guys are, too. It's, um, six p.m. Call me at our house. Okay, so, um, call back soon. And I love you."

I press the button to end the call. I resist the urge to dial the number again just to hear my dad's voice.

Will I ever hear it again?

CHAPTER 37
DAY 2, 7:41 P.M.

When the phone rings, I jump. Ty and I look at each other and then lean over to check the caller ID. The display shows only "Cell Phone," but the number listed is not the number I dialed. My heart is beating in my throat. What if it's Kirk Nowell? With a shaking hand, I pick up the phone.

"Hello?" I make my voice lower and gruffer.

"Cady?" My mom sounds suspicious. "Is that you?"

Hearing her, I melt. "Mom!"

She's still cautious. "What did Grandma give you for Christmas last year?" I can hear the tension in her voice.

I'm sure Mom already knows it's me. So why is she asking? No one but me and my parents would know the real answer to her question. Grandma herself probably wouldn't even remember. If I tell Mom the wrong answer, she'll know I'm under duress.

"Queen-size pantyhose." Mom's mom is known for her

crazy presents, usually purchased at garage sales. I take a deep breath. "Are Dad and Max okay?"

"Basically." Before I can ask Mom what that means, she says quickly, "You need to know that someone is pretending to be your aunt. She's calling herself Elizabeth Quinn, but her real name is Elizabeth Tanzir."

"Mom, we already know about that. She's tied up here at our house, along with Michael Brenner."

"Wait! What? And who's we?"

Ty leans in closer to hear. I pull the phone a half inch from my ear. "There's this guy named Tyler I met in Bend. He's helping me."

"Okay," she says slowly. "Maybe you should start over again from the beginning. Tell me everything that's happened."

I give her an even shorter version than the one I gave Elizabeth, only this one includes my not-so-fatal attack on Brenner, Officer Dillow, "Aunt Liz's" double-cross, and Brenner's broken elbow. I leave in the fugue state but skip over my missing fingernails, knowing they'll just freak Mom out. And I end with, "And right now, they're both tied up in your bedroom."

"You'd better check on them frequently," Mom says. "Especially Elizabeth. And don't trust anything she says."

"Don't worry. She already taught me that." I take a deep breath. "What did you mean when you said Max and Dad were basically all right? Is something wrong?"

Mom sighs and then falls silent. Finally she says, "Yesterday morning, your dad found the proof we needed. Z-Biotech has converted some old storage rooms in the basement. They're raising thousands of infected field mice, but we only need a couple of dozen for legitimate research. They also have a desiccator to dry out the droppings, which basically turns them into a bioweapon. Your dad took photos of the mice and the desiccator, and then he took a sample of the desiccated droppings. He called me and told me we had to leave in a hurry. I grabbed up Max from day care and met your father in the back parking lot. But Kirk tried to stop us. Your dad ended up getting shot." Over my gasp, she hurries to tell me the rest. "It went through his shoulder without hitting anything vital. But he's lost a lot of blood."

"Why didn't you take him to the hospital? Or go to the police?"

"First, we wanted to make sure you were safe. We called your phone, but you didn't pick up. We called the school, but they told us you weren't in class. That's when we knew things had gone wrong, and we left you that message to give you a way to contact us if you could. We bought a couple of disposable phones a few months ago in case we needed them. We didn't realize until later that Kirk had left us messages on our old phones telling us he had you. And that he would kill you if we went to the authorities."

"You talked to him?" I think of his voice, so calm as he punched me in the jaw. So reasonable even when he put the gun between my eyes.

"Just called in later to listen to the messages. He left us several and in one"—her voice breaks—"and in one . . . oh, Cady . . . it was just you screaming. He told us if we wanted to see you alive again, we had to meet you at the cabin. But by the time we heard the message, the deadline he had given us had already passed. I left your father with Max, and I took the gun and went to the cabin to try to rescue you. But instead, it was on fire. And when we heard on the radio that there were human remains . . ." Mom's voice breaks.

"It was actually a chimp, I guess, one from the lab. The same one they tried to make me think was Max." I take a deep breath. "So we can go to the police now, right? I think the main station is downtown. Let's meet there."

"Cady," she says, and then stops. "That's the other thing. We were in a hurry when we left. Your dad was in the back seat with Max, trying to stop the bleeding while I drove. I tossed him the first-aid kit from the glove compartment, and he was ripping open packages of bandages. He also had the sample in a vial in a bag, and we think Max must have been trying to help by opening things up. Maybe he thought it was some kind of medicine." Her voice shakes. "Max has been exposed to the hantavirus."

My heart stops beating. I know what she's going to say next.

"We only realized it today when we found the vial un-capped in the back seat. That means we have just about a day to give Max the vaccine. Once he starts showing symptoms, there will be nothing anyone can do."

I try to imagine Max pale and listless, coughing up blood between violet lips. But instead I just remember him in his tub, lining up his shampoo bottles shaped like Tigger and Eeyore and Pooh, offering them drinks of bathwater from a blue plastic cup.

And then I run through what Mom just said one more

time. "What about you guys? If Max is exposed, doesn't that mean you are, too?"

"When the animal tests went well, people at the lab volunteered to be part of the preliminary clinical human trials before we ramped up vaccine production. So your dad and I are okay, at least as far as being exposed goes. We're already immune. But we have to get our hands on the vaccine for Max. We can't go back there ourselves. I'm sure our security cards have already been deactivated and our pictures are posted at the front desk."

"You mean you want me to go . . ." I let my words trail off.

"Yes. To Z-Biotech. You can use Elizabeth's ID to get in."

"Why can't we just tell the police what happened and make them get it for us?"

"We can't take that chance, Cady. The window is already closing. What if Kirk decides to destroy the vaccine?" I hear the despair in my mom's voice, how thin the edge is between her and a breakdown. "If he knew that Max had been exposed, he would do it just to punish us."

There must be a way that won't involve going in the lion's den. "Don't you know how to make the vaccine yourself?"

"It takes months to grow. Even the batch that's in production now won't be done for another week. Max has to have it by tomorrow or it will be too late."

I think of the guy Elizabeth told us about, the one who died on the way to his girlfriend's funeral. Who drowned in his own blood. Then I take a deep breath.

"What can I do?"

CHAPTER 38
DAY 2, 8:54 P.M.

At Home Depot, it takes what's left of Ty's money plus most of what we took from Elizabeth's purse and Brenner's wallet to buy a janitor's cart, cleaning supplies, an industrial-size broom, two sets of dark blue coveralls, two painter's caps, and a yellow sign that warns in English and Spanish about wet floors.

On our way out, I spot a pay phone. I tell the girl who answers the phone at Fast Fitness that the car that was stolen from their lot earlier in the day is now in the parking garage of the Winchester Hotel in Portland. I hang up when she starts asking questions.

I hurry back to where Ty is unloading the cart. What we really need is a van, but what we've got is Elizabeth's Avalon. We barely manage to squeeze everything in the trunk, and that's only by folding down the back seat. It takes two tries to get the lid closed. Then, still standing in the parking lot, we pull the coveralls on over our clothes.

Ty and I are going to be the new cleaning service for Z-Biotech. We're hoping that Kirk Nowell is more worried about taking care of loose ends than he is about protecting his home base. According to Mom, Elizabeth's employee ID badge should get us in the front door as well as into any of the locked rooms we need to visit. Everyone at Z-Biotech has a certain level of security, but Elizabeth's clearance is the highest level. Her ID badge will let us into everything, from the gate around the parking lot to the front door to all the laboratory spaces. Once we're in the building, there's just one security guard at night, and Mom's pretty sure he spends most of his time sitting at the front desk doing Sudoku.

"Do you know any Spanish?" I ask Ty as I take the on-ramp for the freeway.

"*Si. Un poco.*"

I think that means, "Yes, a little." And with his dark hair and eyes, Ty could be Hispanic.

"Then you should be the one to talk to the security guy. But mostly in Spanish." I remember the cleaners I've seen in various public bathrooms. All of them seem to have come from other, poorer countries. "My French won't sound right."

I grip the steering wheel harder and straighten up. It's hard to believe that it's been less than two days since I returned home for my phone and walked into a nightmare. Hard to believe that I've known Ty for only about a day. I'm wired and tired, so tired I probably shouldn't be driving. I take another slug of the four-shot Venti-size mocha I got from the Starbucks next to the Home Depot. We used the last of the money to buy coffees and muffins. The muffins were gone before we got back to the car.

The industrial area where Z-Biotech is located is deserted at night. The building sits in the middle of a parking lot, which is surrounded by a tall, metal fence topped with razor wire. I hold my breath when I put Elizabeth's ID card up to the reader in front of an automatic rolling gate, but after a second or two, it rattles open and then closes behind us. The parking lot is empty, except for a small orange pickup with silver duct tape holding up one side of the bumper. Ty nudges me and points at the white letters on the tailgate that spell out D-A-T-S-U-N. It seems like a sign. I hope it's a good one.

We park at the far edge of the lot, out of sight of the glass front door. I pull my cap low, and we get out of the car. After we load up the janitor's cart, Ty begins to push it toward the door. At every step, the gun digs into my belly. Ty also has a gun tucked into his waistband.

The brown plastic box of a second card reader is mounted to the left of the glass door. In the lobby, a short, round man with a bald head and a close-cropped black beard sits at a desk. He is staring down at a thin paperback, his pen poised. He hasn't seen us yet.

I'm the cleaner, I tell myself. My name is Ilsa. We're here because we underbid Z-Biotech's last janitorial service. The only way we'll make a living is to work thirteen hours straight, seven days a week. America is not like I thought. My hands are red and rough, even though I wear the yellow rubber gloves.

The guard doesn't even look up until the door clicks as Ty waves Elizabeth's ID card over the reader.

"Hey," he says as Ty walks in and I follow, bumping the cart over the threshold. "What are you guys doing here?" He pushes back from the desk and stands up. He's got a belt that holds a half dozen black holsters and cases, but not, as far as I can see, one for a gun.

"*Nuevo* cleaning service," Ty says, with a sort-of Spanish accent. He hefts the broom to underline what he's saying. I stare at the carpet, think about my cracked hands, about how I'm looking forward to going home and putting my feet up.

The security guard still looks uncertain, but Ty is already heading back toward the hall. We're almost all the way there when I see the man pick up the phone. And suddenly I'm no longer Ilsa. I'm Cady, and I've got a gun in my hand, and I'm barking, "Put down the phone!"

The guard is as slow to react to my command as he was to decide there was something wrong with us. For a long moment I wonder what I'll do if he actually starts punching numbers.

But the phone finally clunks back into its cradle. The guard raises his hands. "Please don't hurt me," he says, his voice shaking.

"Just do what we say, and everything will be all right." Through an open door behind him, I see what looks like a small conference room, with a half dozen chairs around an empty table. "Get in there," I say, gesturing with the gun. Ty pushes the cart with one hand while he grabs the twist of thin yellow nylon rope we bought at Home Depot with the other.

The guard walks ahead of us. There are already half moons of sweat under the arms of his light blue uniform shirt. I wonder how much he knows about what really goes on here, or if he knows anything.

While I hold the gun, Ty quickly searches the guard. He tosses the equipment belt and the contents of his pockets onto the cart, and then ties him up. The final step is to wrench the phone from the wall, the way we did at my house. We're getting to be old hands at this, so it doesn't even take that long.

We push the cart down the long hall, past the large room that holds the primary-colored toys and plastic furniture of the day care, then past a small cafeteria and a few offices. When we reach the elevator, I press the button for the third floor. Where my mom said the vaccine is, the vaccine Max needs to live.

CHAPTER 39
DAY 2, 9:22 P.M.

The first time I was in a lab was when I was twelve and came here for Take Your Daughter to Work day. Now that I've had high school chemistry, I know how impressive Z-Biotech's lab area is. Computers, gleaming microscopes, glass barriers with glove inserts, rows of glassware from tiny bottles to big beakers, stainless steel sinks operated by foot pedals, and hoods to keep any airborne contaminants from leaking into the room.

Tyler takes an audible breath. "The air seems weird in here."

I wonder if he's thinking of the masks and gloves we chose not to put on. My mom said we didn't need them, and I want to be in and out of here as fast as possible.

"There's negative airflow. It keeps the air coming inside the room instead of going out." If there was any kind of spill in here, it wouldn't spread through the vents to the rest of the building.

Rows of stainless steel doors line two of the walls. But not all of them belong to coolers I realize as I pull open the third one over and warm, moist air rolls out. Inside are racks and racks of white eggs.

Ty whistles. "So each one of those eggs has been injected with hantavirus?"

"I guess so." Despite the warm air, I shiver. "How long did Elizabeth say it takes to grow the vaccine?"

"Months, wasn't it?"

Ty's eyes meet mine. It's like we're sharing the same thought. We're here to get the finished vaccine for Max, but if Z-Biotech can't offer this vaccine after it's finished growing, then it can't put its plan into place.

I close the door, then tap the temperature gauge above the warmer. "Look at this sensor. The eggs have to be incubated at a certain temperature. Three degrees hotter and they'll go into a danger zone."

Ty squints. "I think that's three degrees Celsius. Do you know what that is in Fahrenheit?"

"Six? Ten? Whatever it is, it can't be that much. And then they'll start to cook."

I start scrabbling around on the janitor's cart where Ty dumped the contents of the guard's pockets. I remember seeing a red and white pack of Marlboros, so there must be a lighter, right? At first, I'm looking for something lightweight, plastic and colorful, but I don't find it amid the coins, sticks of gum, and car keys. Then I realize what the guard really has is an old silver Zippo. I flip open the lid and thumb the wheel. A bright orange flame appears.

Ty and I grin at each other. Then I snap the lid closed, snuffing the flame.

Ty lifts the shredder off a wastebasket sitting next to one of the desks and starts pulling out handfuls of paper confetti, perfect for feeding a fire.

"How do you like your eggs?"

"Hard cooked." I smile. "You get that going while I find the finished vaccine for Max. And then let's get out of here."

At the other end of the room, I pull open the third door from the left, the one where my mom said I would find the vaccine. This time it's a real cooler. The shelves are crowded. I push small plastic bottles from one side to the other. With every second, my anxiety level increases. What if they moved the vaccine to another room? What if someone has knocked it over or used it up? My mom thought it was on the top shelf, but I don't find it there. Not on the second either. It's not until I check the third shelf that I find it. It doesn't look like much, just a clear plastic bottle with a handwritten label that reads HV VACCINE. Suddenly, the band that's been constricting my heart loosens.

I'm ready to drop it into the insulated lunch bag we brought from home to keep the vaccine cool, but my thoughts keep turning. When the first workers show up tomorrow, they'll untie the security guard. And Nowell will hear about how two teens broke in. He'll know who we are. What he won't know is why we were here, why we came to the last place he'd expect us to be. He'll hunt for clues explaining why we were here by looking for what's missing. If he figures out it's the vaccine, he might guess it's my brother who's in trouble. He knows my parents are already vaccinated.

The less Nowell knows or guesses, the better. I need to throw him off the trail. I think of a plan.

A minute later, I hear a door close. I think it's Ty shutting the door to the warmer, but when I turn to look at him, his expression is frozen. I know, even before I follow his gaze, that we're in big trouble.

A man is standing in the doorway, holding a gun. With a swept-back mane of silver hair, he's dressed in a well-cut dark suit that goes a long way to hiding his bulk. I look down at his feet. At the sight of his oxblood shoes, my blood chills.

He smiles at me, a smile that stops before it reaches his cold gray eyes. "Well, hello, Cady. Like a bad penny, you just keep turning up. Only this time you've brought a friend." Kirk Nowell's familiar voice sounds cheerful. It's the voice of a morning TV show host. But the look in his eyes gives him away, calculating and mean.

"I have a little problem," Nowell says. "Elizabeth isn't answering her phone. And yet she's here at the lab in the middle of the night. When she's supposed to be getting you to reveal your parents' whereabouts. And then I realized that someone must be using her ID badge."

"How did you know anyone was here?" I ask. My voice pleases me. It's as calm as his.

His laugh sounds like something breaking. With his free hand, he taps a phone protruding from his breast pocket. "There's an app for that." The false smile leaves his face.

My expression doesn't change. I won't let him see how afraid I am. Not just for me but for Max and Ty. If I don't bring back the vaccine, Max will die.

The only reason I won't bring back the vaccine is if I'm dead myself.

Which seems just like the kind of thing Nowell wants.

I can already imagine him adding another chapter to the story he's been writing about me. He'll say I broke in here looking for animal tranquilizers or stuff to steal, and that during a confrontation he was forced to kill me and the one-step-up-from-homeless guy I had picked up along the way. And after he's managed to hunt down and really kill my brother as well as my parents, he'll work out a way to make it look like I did that, too. Killed them as part of my drug-addled spree. Just like I supposedly killed Officer Dillow.

His voice interrupts my thoughts. "You must have Michael's and Elizabeth's guns. Pick them up by the barrels and put them on the floor. Now." He swivels his own gun to point it at Ty. "Or I shoot him in the head."

I have no doubt that he means what he says. And while there must be something we could do—some tricky move that would both distract him and leave us unscathed—I can't think of what it is. We both reach under our coveralls. Nowell's expression doesn't change, but I can see his finger tighten infinitesimally on the trigger. A second later, the two guns are on the floor. Leaving us what for weapons? A mop? A broom?

"So why are you two here?" Nowell says thoughtfully. "Why would you risk everything to come here? And to this room in particular. Not the room where the hantavirus is being manufactured. The room your father found because he couldn't leave well enough alone." His face changes as understanding dawns. "When your father left, he stole a sample. Did something happen to that sample? Did someone become contaminated?"

There's no point in lying anymore. "It's Max."

"So it's been"—Nowell's eyes flick upward, thinking, but are back to me before I can make any kind of move— "what? Thirty-six hours? That means late tomorrow your little brother will start running a fever that just keeps climbing. And his back and hips will ache like someone's trying to tear the meat from his bones. Then his lungs will begin to fill with blood, and he'll struggle for breath. Have you ever seen anyone die like that? It's not pretty. They panic, like a drowning swimmer, but there's nothing you can do because they're drowning from the inside, and there's no medicine that can save them. And finally he'll die. Your little brother will die, and there'll be nothing you and your parents will be able to do but watch."

"Not if we get him the vaccine," I say. *Don't act. Be.* I'm another person now, an even more desperate version of me. Max's life depends on it. "Please. Max is only three years old. He doesn't know anything. He can't hurt you in any way. Just let him live. Let me bring the vaccine to him, and after that I don't care what happens to me."

Nowell's reply is full of lilting sarcasm. "He doesn't know anything, just like you didn't know anything? Your parents have already taught me what happens when I trust someone in your family. They could have been rich beyond their wildest imaginings. And no one would have been hurt. People would have paid well to make sure that didn't happen. It was simply a matter of wealth transference."

As he speaks, he moves toward the third cooler. The cooler with the container labeled HV VACCINE. Still keeping the gun trained on us, he opens it, reaches in with one hand, and unerringly finds the bottle.

"No, I'm sorry, Cady, but I can't let you take this. Your parents knew there would be a price if they went against me. Now they have to be prepared to pay it." He takes the bottle I just had within my grasp, and in one motion he unscrews the cap with his thumb.

"No!" I scream. Before I can get to him, he laughs and pours it down the sink. I slap my palm over the drain, but it's all seeped away. The bottle is empty.

And Nowell is laughing. Laughing as I scream.

Behind us, an alarm begins to sound, an unending high-pitched drone. Nowell's head whips around. Smoke is seeping from under the warmer door.

"What have you done?" His voice is nearly drowned out by the alarm. "What have you idiots done?"

Nowell runs over and grabs the handle of the warmer. But when he wrenches open the door, a flash of orange explodes out. A fireball envelops him, rolling up and over his body. And then everything goes dark.

CHAPTER 40
DAY 3, 5:07 A.M.

When I wake up, I'm lying on my back on a narrow bed made with white linens. The ceiling is white acoustical tile and the walls are pale green. It's the third time in a row I've woken up someplace I didn't recognize. First the cabin. Then Ty's bedroom. Now I guess it's a hospital room.

Only this time my mom is asleep in a chair next to me. When I sit up, she starts awake. Her eyes dart around the room, and then she takes a deep, shaky breath and hugs me so hard I can't breathe. But I don't mind.

"Max?" I ask her when she finally loosens her grip. My voice is a croak. She pulls back but keeps her hands on my shoulders.

"It looks like he'll be okay. Thanks to you, Cady." Mom kisses my cheek and then takes my good hand in hers. I notice that they are both bandaged, not just the one with the missing fingernails. "He got the vaccine a couple of hours ago."

"He did?" I realize it's still dark outside. Still nighttime.

"You were so smart, Cady"—violet shadows lie under her eyes—"switching the vaccine to an unmarked bottle and putting it in the insulated lunch bag. That kept it cool when the fire flashed over. Nowell thought he poured the vaccine down the drain, but it was really just a vial of water. Max is running a little bit of a fever, and they're monitoring him, but so far, it's just a precaution." She takes a shaky breath. "I was so worried I had lost both of you. I don't think I could live if I did."

"And Daddy?" The word slips out. I haven't called him Daddy since I was Max's age. But I feel like a little kid. I want to be a little kid again, when my parents could keep me safe.

Mom blinks a few times, but before I can get too worried she gently squeezes my shoulder and says, "He had to have some surgery and now they've got him on IV antibiotics because of the wound in his shoulder. But he should be okay, too."

"And Ty? The guy who was helping me?" He was closer to Nowell when Nowell opened the door.

"He's got some first- and second-degree burns, like you. And like you, they say he'll be okay." She leans down and hugs me again. "Oh, Cady, we're so lucky to have you as a daughter," she whispers in my ear. "You saved us. You saved us all."

We're both quiet for a long moment. I'm trying to take in that it's all over. Really over. Everyone is safe.

"What happened? All we were doing was trying to heat up the eggs so that Nowell wouldn't be able to use the virus inside them to make a vaccine. We lit a fire and closed the door to the warmer. But when he opened the door, it exploded."

"I guess it's called a backdraft. The fire had been starved of oxygen and then got a fresh supply when Kirk pulled the door open. Thank God the building is new enough that it has a sprinkler system. It could have been much worse."

I remember angry orange flames, the gray smoke that suddenly rolled over me. Screaming Ty's name, I had dropped to the floor. And that's the last thing I really remember. I have fainter memories of water falling like rain, sirens, people lifting me up.

"How did the firemen know to come?"

"The fire triggered the sprinklers, and the sprinkler system automatically notified the fire department and told them which floor the fire was on," Mom says. "When the firefighters found the security guard tied up, they called the police. Nowell was still holding a gun, and Ty was able to tell them something about what was going on. Now Homeland Security is investigating."

"And Nowell? Is he dead?"

"Kirk's got second-degree flash burns, and he's lost his hair and eyebrows. I understand he has some upper airway issues due to the heat of the gases. But he'll live. Which I guess is a good thing." Mom gives me a crooked smile. "And Elizabeth and Michael are in custody."

I don't know whether to be glad or sorry that Nowell is alive. The rest is very good. And suddenly my eyes are so heavy that I have to close them again.

But this time I know I'm safe.

CHAPTER 41

THREE MONTHS LATER

Next to me, Ty sticks out his tongue and tips his head back, balancing on his ski poles. He's trying to catch one of the fat flakes that are beginning to drift down from the pale sky. The woods around us are deserted, just sparkling snow and dark evergreens and the faint tracks left by our cross-country skis. Even though being here was Ty's suggestion, I worried it would remind him too much of his dad's accident. But we're on cross-country skis, sticking to groomed trails and keeping well away from the trees.

"Gah one!" Ty snaps his mouth shut and raises his head to look at me, grinning.

"It's amazing to think each one is different." With the fingertip of my glove, I nudge a snowflake that has just landed on the sleeve of my turquoise down jacket. It shimmers and then turns into a rivulet of water.

"Just like people."

"And fingerprints," I say with a shiver. It's about twenty degrees outside, cold enough that each breath is sharp in my nose. But that isn't why I can feel gooseflesh walking up my arms underneath my thick wool sweater.

Fingerprints make me think of criminals, which makes me think of Kirk Nowell, Elizabeth Tanzir, and Michael Brenner. All three are in jail and have been denied bail after having been deemed flight risks. Their trials won't take place until summer. There's another half dozen guys who helped hunt for me and my parents, but they're busy cutting deals with the prosecutors. Nowell is facing the most serious charges, including murder for shooting poor Officer Dillow.

Nowell tracked me to Newberry Ranch (and later to Ty's apartment) through Brenner's work-issued cell phone, which had a built-in GPS. Like James had guessed, Nowell used a spoof card to make Officer Dillow think he was calling from Sagebrush. Brenner is the one who hacked into Facebook and put up my fake profile and status updates.

Ty sees me shiver. "Cold?" He shifts one of his ski poles, puts his arm around me, and runs his hand up and down my arm. Is he just being nice, or does it mean something more? We've been texting each other a few times a day, but living in different cities, we've hardly spent any time together since the police finished questioning us. Ty came to Portland last month when we were part of a big award ceremony held by the governor. We were surrounded by hero cops and hero firefighters. All those folks in uniform got to their feet and applauded us for stopping Z-Biotech's plan.

Now, three months after everything happened, our lives have mostly returned to normal. We're both back at school and complaining about homework. I'm not on the cover of magazines anymore, and I no longer have to worry about turning on the TV and hearing my name. When the man whose car we stole heard the whole story, he decided not to press charges.

We came here this weekend so my parents could talk to contractors about having a new cabin built on the same site. They had asked me if they should sell it, wondered if the bad memories would overwhelm me. But now that I have my memory back, I know there are so many more good memories. Plus there's Ty himself, only forty-five minutes away.

He squeezes my shoulder, and I realize he's still waiting for an answer.

"I've been having a lot of bad dreams lately."

In my dreams, the fire still explodes out of the stainless steel door, but it's Max who had opened it. In the worst of the dreams, Max is dead and Kirk Nowell is coming at me with a pair of pliers. Or Max is sick, bright red blood frothing on his lips, and I hold his tiny body until it goes limp and his eyes roll back in his head. No matter what form the nightmare takes, I wake up feeling drained, bile bitter on the back of my tongue.

The government is now making a new batch of the hantavirus vaccine. The plan is for it to be ready by next summer so they can offer it to the farmers and ranchers who live in the area where the field mice make their home. My parents are working with other virologists and wildlife biologists to figure out if it's possible to eliminate the hantavirus from the field mice altogether.

Ty drops his arm, shrugs his backpack onto one shoulder, and pulls out a thermos. "I've got the cure for bad dreams," he says. "Hot cocoa."

"With marshmallows?" I'm joking, but he grins and pulls a plastic bag of mini marshmallows from one of his coat pockets.

While he unscrews the lid, I try to shake away the memories, to ground myself in the moment. We're safe now, and free, and we're no longer on the run. I know who I am and I have all my memories—good and bad. When the trials happen, I'll deal with them.

I take a deep breath of the sharp, clean air. The snow sparkles in the sun like diamonds. Ty hands me the tiny tan plastic cup, and I fill my mouth with the sweet brown liquid, the marshmallows melting on my tongue. I feel the warmth going all the way down.

I hand the empty cup back to Ty. He fills it again and raises it to his mouth, his eyes scanning the horizon, while I watch him. I'm not sure how I should act around him. Everything has been so crazy. We know all kinds of things about each other, and we know we can trust each other, but we've never kissed. Does he even like me as a girl? Does he even know the real me? And who is the real me anyway? The girl who got straight As and starred in plays? The girl who almost died? The girl who fought back any way she could?

And then Ty turns to me and his lips touch mine. And I find an old answer deep within myself.

Don't act. Be.

The past is over; the future is yet to come. I have only this moment, sparkling like a diamond in my hand and then melting like a snowflake.

I stop thinking and kiss him back.

ACKNOWLEDGMENTS

Thanks to Christy Ottaviano, Amy Allen, Marianne Cohen, Rich Deas, April Ward, Holly Hunnicutt, Allison Verost, Lucy Del Priore, Emily Waters, and all the other wonderful folks at Henry Holt/Macmillan. I am so glad you are on my team. My agent, Wendy Schmalz, has been my cheerleader, advocate, and confidant for twenty years.

Firefighter and paramedic Joe Collins helped me figure out how to best set a fire. Dr. Denene Lofland shared her knowledge of bioweapons. Author Jennifer Lynn Barnes answered a weird question I had about chimpanzees. And a police officer who would rather not be named was kind enough to send me snapshots of the inside of her patrol car.

Thanks also to two all-around-wonderful resources: Lee Lofland, who founded The Writers Police Academy, and all the great experts in the Crime Scene Writers Yahoo Group.

Singer-songwriter Kathleen Edwards inadvertently sparked the idea for this book.

And without my family, none of this would be worthwhile.

GOFISH

APRIL HENRY

© Randy Patten

What did you want to be when you grew up?
An ophthalmologist. Why? I have no idea. Maybe because it's so hard to spell.

When did you realize you wanted to be a writer?
Initially I thought about being a writer when I was nine or ten. Then I lost my courage and didn't find it again until I was about thirty.

What's your most embarrassing childhood memory?
People used to call me Ape, and I did a pretty good monkey impression. The trick is to put your tongue under your upper lip and scrunch up your nose while making chimp noises. Only now, looking back on it, I'm embarrassed to think about it.

What's your favorite childhood memory?
When I was ten, I asked for nothing but books for Christmas. After we unwrapped our presents, I went back into bed and read.

SQUARE FISH

As a young person, who did you look up to most?

Roald Dahl, who wrote *Charlie and the Chocolate Factory*. I wrote him letters and sent him stories, and he sent me back a couple of postcards. I still have one that complimented my story about a six-foot-tall frog named Herman who loved peanut butter.

What was your favorite thing about school?

English and math, but I liked nearly all subjects. If life were like school, I would be a millionaire. Unfortunately for my bank account, real life and school only overlap to a certain extent.

What was your least favorite thing about school?

PE. I was the clumsiest person imaginable. I hurt my knee on the pommel horse, bruised my inner arm from wrist to elbow in archery, and sank when I was supposed to be swimming.

What were your hobbies as a kid? What are your hobbies now?

I read or hung out with my friends. We lived near a cool old cemetery, and sometimes we would even go sledding or picnic there.

Now I run, read, and practice kajukenbo, a mixed marital art. We even spar—and I'm pretty good. If only my old PE teacher, Miss Fronk, could see me now.

What was your first job, and what was your "worst" job?

My first job was at a library in the children's section. I used to hide in the stacks and read Judy Blume when I was supposed to be shelving books.

My worst job was at a bank. A monkey who knew the alphabet could have done that job—and would probably have had a better time.

How did you celebrate publishing your first book?

I stink at celebrating. I did buy a pair of earrings.

Where do you write your books?

On my couch, at the coffee shop, in the library, at the car fix-it place (where I am a lot).

What sparked your imagination for *The Girl Who Was Supposed to Die*?

For the past few years, I've been writing books inspired by real events. I'll hear something on the news and I'll think, Hmm, what if . . . ? That's where *Girl, Stolen* and *The Night She Disappeared* came from. But *The Girl Who Was Supposed to Die* was actually inspired by the lyrics to a song called "Scared at Night" by Kathleen Edwards. In the song, a character accidentally injures the barnyard cat while he's shooting at rats. His dad tells him he has to take the cat out back and finish it off.

One day when I was running, I was listening to this on my iPod shuffle, and I thought, Ooh—what if there was a girl? And she wakes up on the floor of a ransacked cabin with two men standing over her. And one of them says, "Take her out back and finish her off."

The more I ran, the more I thought about it, and the more I knew she had been tortured and the two men were mad because she wouldn't—couldn't—tell them something they really wanted to know.

Have you ever had amnesia?

No. That would be awful! For years, though, I've been collecting stories of people who experience fugue-state amnesia. In 1985, a Tacoma reporter disappeared. A lot of people thought she had been murdered in connection with a story. She turned up twelve years later in Sitka, Alaska, with no memory of her past life. In 2009, a school teacher disappeared for three weeks in Manhattan. When authorities went back and looked at security cam footage, they would see her going into a store, for example, looking confused and eventually leaving. When she was found, she had no memory of who she was.

People suffering from a fugue state cannot recall their past. They don't lose their memory of how to function in the world—they just lose their personal memories. There's a fascinating British documentary about a guy who walked into a hospital and said he had no idea who he was. In one amazing scene he goes to the beach. He's standing on a rock next to the water and he says, "I don't know if I know how to swim. I guess I'll find out!" And then he jumps.

One thing people with fugue state seem to have in common is that they have been under immense stress. One theory is that some brains, when subjected to a lot of stress, simply hit the reboot key. It's a way for the person to run away from a bad situation.

When my fictional girl wakes up in this trashed cabin, she realizes someone has pulled out two of her fingernails.

She figures that's what has caused her to lose her memory. But it's actually something worse—much worse.

Did you have to do any research for this book?
One thing I had to do was figure out why the bad guys wanted to kill my main character. And I had to figure out if she might possibly be crazy—and I definitely wanted her to look crazy.

I spent a lot of time researching bioweapons. It's illegal to manufacture them, but it's not illegal to research how to defend against one, which is a pretty big loophole. I stocked an imaginary lab, looked at online catalogs, debated the merits of special cages that can hold a thousand mice, figured out how to grow a virus and make a vaccine. I spent so much time researching bioweapons, it's a wonder the FBI didn't come knocking at my door. My fictional world was reviewed by a scientist who has a top-security clearance and has done bioweapons research. She said the idea was "very plausible—and evil."

Was anything in the story inspired by something in your life?
What would you do if someone tried to drag you into the woods to kill you? Well, what I did was have my kajukenbo instructor drag me around the floor with his hands under my armpits. Then we figured out some ways the girl could fight back.

I'm now taking kung fu, and both martial arts have really helped me construct fight scenes and understand the sheer physicality of violence. The only downside is that doctors often look at the fingerprint-shaped bruises on my arms and ask if I'm safe at home.

If you were on the run, what are the most important items you would take with you?

A lot of money would be good. Photos of my family. Actually, I would want my family, so I would probably get caught. If you really want to go on the run, you have to cut all ties with your past for good. You have to stop doing the things you used to do, and lead a completely different and quiet life.

What do you hope readers take away from this book?

I just want them to get lost in the fun of the story. Oh, and to think about learning a martial art.

What's your favorite thriller movie?

Three Days of the Condor.

What challenges do you face in the writing process, and how do you overcome them?

Deadlines are the biggest challenge. You just have to take them one day at a time.

Which of your characters is most like you?

All of my characters have a little bit of me in them. Even the killers.

What makes you laugh out loud?

Failblog.org.

What do you do on a rainy day?

Rainy or overcast days are a part of everyday life in Portland. I do pretty much what I do on any day. The hardest thing to do is to go out the door for a run when it's pouring. Once you get started, it's not so bad, but a GORE-TEX jacket is essential.

What's your idea of fun?

Hanging out with my writing friends. Opening a book that has been getting really great reviews. And sparring. I love to spar. It makes me feel powerful to see a guy flinch.

Who is your favorite fictional character?

A guy named Rusty in a Scott Turow book. He is a liar and a cheat, and as a reader you really like him. I'm still not sure how Scott Turow pulled that off.

What was your favorite book when you were a kid? Do you have a favorite book now?

I loved *The Silver Crown* by Robert C. O'Brien. I have read so many books that I don't have one favorite—I have hundreds. *The Hunger Games* was great, as was *Life As We Knew It.*

What's your favorite TV show or movie?

I really like *Breaking Bad,* which is dark, dark, dark.

If you were stranded on a desert island, who would you want for company?

My teenage daughter. And a person who knows how to use the things you find on a desert island to build a boat.

If you could travel anywhere in the world, where would you go and what would you do?
I would spend a month in Italy looking at ruins and eating pasta.

If you could travel in time, where would you go and what would you do?
I'd like to see what the world would be like in two hundred years' time.

What's the best advice you have ever received about writing?
Tenacity is as important as talent.

Do you ever get writer's block? What do you do to get back on track?
I force myself to write. You can't edit nothing. Or sometimes I'll jump ahead and write a part I was looking forward to writing.

What would you do if you ever stopped writing?
Die.

What do you like best about yourself?
If I see a need, I try to meet it.

Do you have any strange or funny habits? Did you when you were a kid?
When I'm bored, I catch myself making a cloverleaf tongue. My teenager has been able to make one since she was little, and once when I was bored I taught myself

how. It's supposed to be a rare genetic trait, but I think if you can roll your tongue, you can learn how to do it.

What do you consider to be your greatest accomplishment?
My daughter is pretty cool. But she mostly did that on her own.

What do you wish you could do better?
Parallel park. I never really learned how, and now I drive around and around looking for spots I can pull into.

What would your readers be most surprised to learn about you?
Well, then it wouldn't be a surprise, would it? How about—I have one double-jointed thumb. (That's not giving too much away.)

On their first assignment with Portland County's Seach and Rescue team, Alexis, Nick, and Ruby find themselves tasked with finding an autistic man lost in the woods. What they find instead is a dead body. Now they must find the killer before he strikes again.

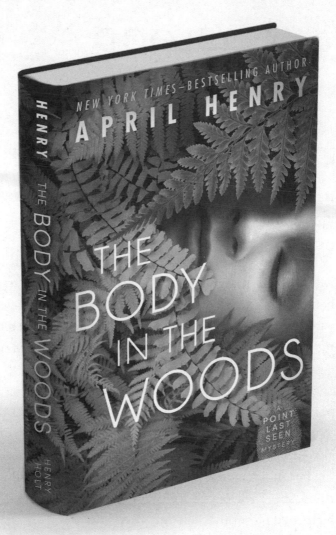

NEW YORK TIMES–BESTSELLING AUTHOR
APRIL HENRY

THE BODY IN THE WOODS

A POINT LAST SEEN MYSTERY

HENRY

THE BODY IN THE WOODS

HENRY HOLT

Turn the page for a sneak peek of

THE BODY IN THE WOODS

BLOOD

OR ALEXIS FROST, NICK WALKER, AND RUBY McClure, it all started with a phone call and two texts. It ended with fear and courage, love and loathing, screaming and blood. Lots of blood.

When the classroom phone rang in American history, Alexis Frost straightened up and blinked, trying to will herself awake as the teacher answered it. She managed to yawn without opening her mouth, the cords stretching tight in her neck. Last night had been another hard one.

"Alexis?" Mrs. Fairchild turned toward her.

"Yes?" Her heart sped up. What was it this time? The possibilities were endless. None of them good.

"Could you come up here, please?"

Mrs. Fairchild was looking at Alexis as if she was seeing her in a new light. Had it finally happened, then, the thing she both feared and longed for? Had something happened to her mother?

Nick Walker's thumbs were poised over the virtual keyboard of the phone he held on his lap. He was pretending to listen to Mr. Dill, his English teacher, while he was really texting Sasha Madigan, trying this angle and that to persuade her to study with him tonight. Which he hoped would mean lots of copying (on his part) and lots of kissing (on both their parts).

The phone vibrated in his hand. Mr. Dill was busy writing on the board, so Nick lifted it a little closer to his face. It wasn't a reply from Sasha but a message from his Portland Search and Rescue team leader.

Search in Forest Park. Missing man. Meet time 1500.

His first SAR call-out! He jumped to his feet.

"Nick?" Mr. Dill turned and looked at him over the top of his glasses. "What is it?" Mr. Dill had a lot of rules. He had already complained about Nick's habit of drawing—only Mr. Dill called it doodling—in class.

Nick held up his phone while pointing at it with his other hand as if he had been hired to demonstrate it. "I'm with Portland Search and Rescue, and we've been mobilized to find a man missing in Forest Park. I have to leave now."

"Um, okay," Mr. Dill said uncertainly. Someone in Wilson High's administration had had to sign off on Nick being allowed to join searches during the school day, but maybe the information hadn't filtered down to his teachers.

No matter. Nick was already out the door.

He just hoped someone from class would tell Sasha. A text wouldn't do it justice.

Nick Walker, called out on a lifesaving mission.

Ruby McClure felt her phone buzz in her jeans pocket. She waited until the end of chemistry to check it.

Fifteen hundred made so much more sense than three P.M. Ruby preferred military time. No questions about whether "nine" meant morning or night. No having to rely on context. No one getting hung up on whether 1200 had an A.M. or a P.M. after it, which was a ridiculous idea because A.M. meant "ante meridiem" and P.M. meant "post meridiem" and *meridiem* was Latin for "midday," and twelve noon was midday itself.

It was 1357 now. Which meant she had an hour to get home, change into hiking clothes, pick up her SAR backpack, and meet the rest of the team at the Portland sheriff's office.

Piece of cake.

Ruby pulled out the keys to her car as she walked to the office to sign herself out. On the way, her phone buzzed again. It was Nick, asking for a ride.

A BUNCH OF TEENAGERS

THE PORTLAND COUNTY SHERIFF'S OFFICE had called out all teams to search for the missing man. Of the twenty teens on Team Alpha, twelve had responded. Now they climbed out of the fifteen-passenger van driven by Jon Partridge, one of the adult advisers, and into a parking lot next to Forest Park. Team Bravo, along with the sheriff's deputy assigned to this search, were in a second van and would take the other end of the huge park. With the exception of the deputy, everyone was a volunteer.

The last one out of the van, Alexis was surreptitiously trying to eat a granola bar from her backpack's emergency rations. Today was looking like it might qualify as an emergency. Not because of this search, but because of how the apartment had looked when she stopped to grab her gear. By the time Alexis had gotten off the city bus at the sheriff's office, the van had been idling outside. She had been the last to board.

Mitchell Wiggins clapped his hands. "Listen up, people!" Mitchell was an Eagle Scout who wanted to be a cop. Even though he had been elected team leader only a few days ago, it was clearly a natural fit. He seemed born to wear some kind of uniform. His yellow SAR climbing helmet—the yellow marked him as the leader, while the rest of the team wore red helmets—was already buckled into place. Now his pale, earnest face regarded each of them in turn. "Today we will be conducting a hasty search for a thirty-four-year-old white man named Bobby Balog."

This was it, then. The real deal. Alexis took a deep breath. Most of the other teens here were certifieds. They had completed the nine months of training and had been called out on dozens of searches. All Alexis and a few of the others had behind them were seven Wednesday-evening classes and two weekend training exercises. From class, she knew that a hasty search was just like it sounded, a quick search that stuck to the most obvious trails and routes. It was also quite possible that this would turn out to be what was known in SAR circles as "a bastard search," when you went looking for someone who was never really lost in the first place.

"Bobby is five foot eight and two hundred pounds," Mitchell continued. "He's wearing dark blue Nike shoes. The sole pattern is made up of squares about the size of keyboard keys." A few of the more experienced kids, who had training in tracking, nodded. "He's also wearing jeans, a gray sweater, and a navy blue windbreaker."

Alexis exchanged a look with Nick. She knew they were thinking the same thing. Not a single bright color. This wasn't going to be easy.

"And he's autistic," Mitchell added, putting the icing on the cake. "The PLS"—point last seen—"is his bedroom, which is a mile from here, but he loves Forest Park and has run away and hidden here before."

"How autistic?" Ruby asked. "That diagnosis covers a wide range of behaviors." She was standing right next to Alexis. Too close. As usual.

Alexis slid a half step sideways. She didn't want anyone thinking they were really friends. Most especially Ruby.

Mitchell was opening his mouth to answer when a silver Lexus sped into the lot. Before it was even at a complete stop, heels were clip-clopping toward them. Their owner was a woman with short, curly dark hair who wore a tailored long black wool coat. Smeared mascara rimmed her red, swollen eyes. Following more slowly in her wake was a silver-haired man dressed in dark slacks, a white shirt, and a black sweater vest. He was coatless, even though the temperature was only in the mid-forties.

"Wait a minute." The woman stopped short when she saw their faces. "*You're* Portland Search and Rescue?"

Mitchell pulled his skinny frame to its full six-foot-two height. "Yes, ma'am, we are."

"A bunch of teenagers?"

"Marla." The man laid his hand on her arm, but she shook it off.

Jon cleared his throat and stepped forward. He might be twenty-six, but Jon had been in SAR since he was fifteen. "Every person you see has volunteered to be here. Most of us have received hundreds of hours of training and conducted dozens of rescues. That's why the Portland County Sheriff's Office chooses us to search for people who are lost or injured." His steel-gray eyes never left the woman's face. "Now, we could keep talking about their experience level, or we could start searching for your son while there's still light."

Mrs. Balog blinked and closed her mouth.

Only Ruby was unfazed by this exchange. "Exactly how autistic is Bobby?"

It was Mr. Balog who answered. "He doesn't have any physical handicaps or other medical conditions. He's a fast walker and not much of a talker. He'll probably hide from you."

"He loves the woods," Mrs. Balog said. "And he doesn't like strangers." She ran a knuckle under one eye. "He's done this twice since we moved to Portland, but the other times it was summer."

Alexis wished they still had summer's long days and warm temperatures. Instead it was November and they were working against time, against the sun that was already sinking, against the night that would drop temperatures even further, against the creeks and fallen snags and rabbit holes that Bobby might blunder into.

Regaining his professional balance, Mitchell turned his focus back to the team. "Remember, guys, your job is not just to search but to inform the public. Let them be your eyes and ears. If they have anything to report, they can do it at the command post we'll set up here."

"I have a photo of Bobby," Mr. Balog offered, pulling a cell phone from his back pocket. His face was creased and worn. Alexis wondered how many of the lines were the result of having a kid who wasn't normal. But you couldn't change your family.

Mitchell took the phone and looked at it for a long moment before passing it on. As it went from hand to hand, Alexis was reminded of the few times her mom had taken her to church, the Communion tray passing in silence. Mrs. Balog shivered as the wind began to pick up, and her husband put his arm around her.

When it was her turn, Alexis cradled the image of Bobby's round face. His smile was strangely wide and flat, as if someone had instructed him to show all his teeth, top and bottom. She silently promised him that she would find him if she could.

Jon's phone rang, and he walked to the other side of the van to answer it. For a second, Alexis strained to hear, wondering if they had found Bobby, but it sounded like he was arguing with his girlfriend. While Jon was busy, Mitchell split them into teams of two or three, assigning the more experienced searchers the higher probability areas. Each team was given a rat pack—a small pack that buckled across the chest and contained a GPS and a radio.

Finally only Alexis, Ruby, and Nick were left to be dispatched. Obviously Alexis should have taken another step away from Ruby while she still had a chance.

Jon came back around the corner of the van. "Where's the rest of the team?"

"Already out on the trail," Mitchell answered.

Jon dropped his voice so the Balogs couldn't overhear. "What were you thinking? These three are brand-new! You should have split them up."

They all looked down the trail, but the others were already out of sight.

Mitchell's face reddened. "Sorry!"

Jon sighed, rubbing a spot just above his left eyebrow. "It is what it is." The Balogs were leaning in, trying to listen, so he lowered his voice slightly. "I don't want you three out of sight of the trail or each other. Nick, you'll be in charge of the rat pack. Ruby, I want you to take the topo map."

Leaving nothing for Alexis. She had tried her best to fit in, but maybe Jon could see right through her.

SAR was her ticket to college. She wasn't going to be like the other girls in her neighborhood, getting pregnant or dropping out or settling for a minimum-wage job. But even a state school would be expensive, and her guidance counselor had told Alexis that her B average was not enough to win her any scholarships. To make herself stand out, the counselor had said, she needed to add an eye-catching extracurricular. But Alexis was too uncoordinated for sports, she couldn't read music, and yearbook had been too competitive.

It had been either this or the Mathletes.

Mitchell handed the topo map to Ruby, and the four of them leaned in close. His long finger traced the way they were supposed to go. "Follow this section of the trail."

"But that's nowhere near where you said he was found the last two times," Nick protested.

Mitchell's jaw clenched. "We need to cover ground, and figuring out where he isn't is almost as important as figuring out where he is. So you guys had better get going."

Suddenly Mrs. Balog grabbed the arm of the blue Gore-Tex jacket Alexis had scored a few weeks ago at Goodwill. "Do you think you'll find him?" Her breath was hot and stale. Alexis couldn't look away from her brown eyes, the whites threaded with red.

What should she say?

"We're going to try."